Love Without Precedence

By
Suzanne Seibel

Dedication

To my husband, Charles, my daughter, Monica, and my sister Michele. The rest of you just need to buy this book…

Copyright 2023 by Suzanne Seibel

Distributed by Kindle Direct Publishing

This is a work of fiction. Names, characters, corporations, institutions, organizations, events, or locals in this novel are either the product of the author's imagination or, if real, used factiously. The resemblance of any character to actual persons (living or dead) is entirely coincidental.

All rights reserved. No part of this book may be reproduced in any form or by any electronic or mechanical means including information storage and retrieval systems—except in the case of brief quotations embodied in critical articles and reviews—without permission.

4

Chapter 1
There's One in Every Condo

Every morning. Every solitary morning that Ashton Walker attempted to depart his condo, headed for his office, he would begin with a peek through the peephole in his front door. He was hoping to find an empty hallway and the apartment door directly across from his own door firmly closed. He was hoping to avoid Doris Pitman, his certifiably obnoxious neighbor, residing in Unit 3D.

Some mornings he was successful. He would open the door to the unpleasant odors of cleaning solutions containing bleach or vinegar. Or the smell of baking brownies, having been left in the oven way too long. But usually it was just a quietness, consistently breached by Mrs. Stubbs' television blaring in her unit down the hallway.

As her age advanced so did the level of Mrs. Stubbs' hearing loss, now exacerbated by the ever-increasing decibels of her television playing almost 24/7. The only time it was turned off was when one of her daughters came to take her to a doctor's appointment or out to lunch. Otherwise it was the muffled drone of a 24-hour news channel or the ticking of the prize wheel on a TV game show, every day, all day.

Ash put his hand on the doorknob, straightened his spine and pulled the white metal door into his apartment…just as Doris Pitman did the same in her mirroring condo unit.

"Ashton," came her usual two-syllable greeting, her gravelly voice revealing years of smoking unfiltered cigarettes.

"Ms. Pitman." He did a quick count of the pink foam rubber curlers in her hair, guesstimating fourteen of them in total.

She projected her cane before her, stepping out onto the matted carpet with its well-worn traffic pattern pointing towards the third-floor elevator. She pulled her door shut, double checking that the lock was set. Making certain his own unit was secured, Ash joined her along the same dirty swath centered on the aged Berber carpet, him too heading for the elevator.

"So, Monday morning. Back to the grind for you." She languidly walked, seeming to be even slower than usual this morning.

"Yes ma'am. Maybe someday I can be retired like you." He politely kept pace although he would have preferred a heated sprint to the steel door, leaving the woman in his dust.

"Oh hogwash, retirement isn't all its cutout to be. I think you will find it very boring, especially as active as you are... all those young ladies in your place every weekend." She even provided a *tsk, tsk, tsk* to punctuate her judgement.

He intercepted her implied meaning. He knew exactly what she thought those young ladies were doing for him in his condo... It wasn't *every* weekend, just most Saturdays. And they weren't doing *that*.

Choosing to ignore her insinuation rather than feed into her contrivance he flatly shared, "I wouldn't mind giving retirement a try for at least a week or two." He refrained from adding, "But I'd probably just become a nosy old bag like you."

Ashton had a leather satchel slung over his shoulder, shifting it upon arrival at the elevator. He pushed the down button and stepped back. The elderly woman on her cane and the young whippersnapper in his dress slacks, lightly starched shirt and stylish tie stood side-by-side before the brushed steel door listening to the hum of the machinery. The door opened and the woman clothed in a floral housecoat entered, barely allowing room for Ash to join her before she turned to face the still open door. Once inside he pushed the illuminated number one, notifying the elevator's cables to take Ms. Pitman to the building's first floor lobby and the bank of resident mailboxes.

"I liked this one," she said as the door closed and the elevator began its descent.

"This one?" He checked his watch.

"Yes, the young lady that was in your condo this weekend."

"Hmm, I'm so glad you approve," he rolled his hazel eyes at the digital numbers clicking off above them.

"The one that was here a couple of weeks ago was very rude. She didn't return my greeting."

Doris clutched the neckline of her housecoat with her free hand giving Ash a look of distrust as he towered above her hunched over figure.

"Well, I'd speak to her about her lack of manners, but she won't be returning. I didn't care for her either."

Ash couldn't resist making an impulsive tilt as if to peer down the old woman's sagging cleavage followed by a nonchalant, open palm smoothing of his hair. She gave him her best evil eye. It had all been so predictable on both of their parts.

Had he ever gotten along with the woman? Had she ever been pleasant? What had he ever done to her to make her so spiteful with him serving as her consistent target?

"No, your girl this weekend was much nicer than that one, but not as nice as the one that was here over Memorial Day weekend. She is my favorite so far. She was so friendly and, and very mannerly."

The door opened and the elderly woman cautiously stepped into the outdated décor of the lobby with its dark wood paneled walls and garish carpet in shades of burnt orange and crimson red. She secured her cane to begin her journey across the lobby to the small mailroom adjacent to the front door of the building. The elevator's doors began to close, to take Ash to his car awaiting in the lower-level parking garage, but not before he heard the elderly woman's testy final shot, taking direct aim at him and his conjectured behavior.

"You might want to get yourself checked for a venereal disease sometime."

Ashton Walker merely lowered his eyes and began to mentally count to one hundred. He found the count was usually sufficient to ward off the impending effects of a spike in his blood pressure and in preventing him from carrying out his malicious plans for the demise of the cantankerous old woman.

***

Ash Walker sat in his office, the door wide open and the sounds of phones buzzing, computer keys clicking and background music smearing all the cacophony into a drone of tolerable noise. He removed the remote control for the electronic window shades from his center desk drawer and brought the sheer gray panels up to block the morning sunlight. He took the pages of documents he had reviewed over the weekend from his satchel and placed them on the empty corner of his desk, sterile in its design. He tossed the satchel beneath the matching credenza behind him, equally as bland in its appearance.

A pile of phone messages sat waiting, centered on the lid of his closed laptop. He took the small stack of yellow post-its and skimmed their messages as he dropped into the high back desk chair. He focused on the names of the senders, ranking their order of importance. On top was a reminder to update his personal information in HR, followed by an invitation to a conference on investing his 401k. A notice that his annual physical was coming due in the next month had the word URGENT in capital letters across the top.

The note from Bernice, the department secretary, was tossed into the trashcan beside his desk. He'd already made a donation to the department's flower fund for the current fiscal year. Ash debated if and when he'd ever be the recipient of a floral acknowledgement from the Legal Department. He decided it would probably be an arrangement of chrysanthemums and gladiolas at his funeral, and therefore wouldn't even be appreciated by him.

He heard the rustle of movement coming through his office door. He looked up to see a woman in stylish slacks and a navy blazer, her hair pulled back in a clump of auburn curls. At least she was carrying two cups of coffee, thrusting one of the throwaway cups at him.

"So, how was this one?" she asked. She lowered herself into one of the faux leather chairs before the desk, attempting to get comfortable in spite of its lack of padding.

"Good. She was good. She followed directions. Did what I liked." Ash removed the cup's plastic lid. He cautiously took a sip, pleasantly surprised that the temperature was just as he liked it. The plastic lid joined the phone message from Bernice in the trashcan.

"Talk too much? Any special talents?" The young woman raised herself up and tried again to find a forgiving position in the chair. She gave another shimmy of her hips, burying her trim buttocks into the seat bottom.

"Nah, all good. Could have been a little more…more willing to try new things … Meet my needs. I have preferences and somethings are just not negotiable."

Finally finding a suitable sag, the woman reclined in the curved back chair. Her eyes proudly read the name plaque centered before him.

Ashton Walker
Attorney at Law
Mergers and Acquisitions

He took a purposeful look-see at his visitor. *How can a male and a female resemble each other so much? Same eye color and shape, same full pouty lips. The lips were probably more attractive on her than on him.*

She brought her paper cup to those lips, taking a small sip. Preceded by an exhausted sigh, "Ash, you need to tell them what you want up front, even before you hand them the money."

"I usually do." He opened the center desk drawer and retrieved two coasters to protect the polished desktop. He took another sip and a sinister grin encroached on his face. "Ms Pitman…" Ash was met with a baffled look from his visitor. "My neighbor…" Now met with a nod of acknowledgement along with a disgruntled supporting themselves and their families. They needed a means to make ends meet and they needed flexibility in doing just that.

She was fortunate in that she had a college education and the moxie to start a business of her own, utilizing the insurance money from her husband's policy. Seeing the policy's payout wasn't sufficient enough to carry her to her own retirement, put their two children through college and allow her to have a leisurely existence until she joined him once again, she realized she'd have to supplement the payout. She would just have to be creative. So she began a cleaning business not as a housekeeper but as an overseer, along with selling franchises of The Cleaning Contessa to other widows around the region.

It also helped that she had a slightly older brother, a corporate lawyer, to guide her in her journey to success. He provided his legal guidance in exchange for a spotless apartment and a homecooked dinner every Thursday evening. Occasionally she'd try to fix him up with a client whom she thought would be a good match with the bachelor, although she was finding her attempts rebuffed more and more lately.

Following a Thursday evening dinner, the brother and sister stationed themselves at the kitchen sink. She washed, he dried. While passing plates and silverware, Meredith attempted to codify what would be the perfect female companion for Ash. The women thus far were deemed too chatty, too introverted, too liberal, too conservative. In pure frustration, Meredith pronounced him to be "too picky."

"I have my own quirks. Why do I need to deal with someone else's?" He saw his sister's bewildered expression. "…Meredith, those women are looking for either the reincarnation of their dead spouse or someone that they can mold into what their ex wasn't."

"Okay… I know, I know. I do exactly that… I'm looking for another Dale."

"Let me do my own shopping for a mate. God knows I have my own bizarre standards."

"Just find someone and soon. You're not getting any younger." Meredith gave a shove to her big brother.

Meredith had found a passion for doing the actual hiring and training of potential housekeepers. This way she could make certain a high level of quality was in place, the job was being done right, and the business's reputation maintained. When she felt the trainees were almost ready to leave the nest, she would send the rookie housekeepers to the home of her brother for a trial run. Just recently, she had interviewed a couple of male candidates interested in pursuing the position usually considered degradingly menial and feminine in nature, but now paying quite well in the current economy.

God knows what Doris would think if there was a male knocking on Ash's front door on a Saturday morning.

Chapter 2

Hit On at the HOA Meeting

Removing a legal guide from the bookcase in his office, Ash began his day as a lawyer for PaseoParkTechnology, a recognized and well-respected computer technology firm headquartered in Kansas City, Missouri. He specialized in the mergers and acquisitions of smaller technology companies into the ever-growing conglomerate. This usually entailed the smaller firm losing its identity and being totally absorbed by the bigger fish. Ash had likened the process to getting married with the changing of the name and the divvying-up of responsibilities. He also likened the process to those marriages that suffered from domestic violence, the spouse being controlling, even abusive.

Occasionally, smaller technology firms would seek out the technology powerhouse for a buyout, only to be told they weren't ready for such a merger, to come back when they had more experience, more clients, and more accrued wealth. And other companies were made offers they couldn't refuse, either because the buyout was so lucrative or they would be underbid and driven to their knees, finding themselves with no choice but to merge with PaseoParkTechnology.

There were times when Ash would be required to strong arm a reluctant seller, one who just wanted a run at the crown held by PaseoParkTechnology. He would try to be polite and to be fair in his dealings. That was until his boss would

"Wow, old people. What keeps you there? Do you have a swimming pool? A workout room? A concierge?" The two young men walked down the corridor of desks, towards the bank of elevators for the office building. Both turned to locate the vile odor of someone eating tuna fish at their desk. They were met with a snarling face, the clerk obviously not enjoying their lunch either.

"No. None of that. There are no perks. It's just twelve units and eleven senior citizens smelling up the place with analgesics for arthritis and garlic rubs." He had a flash back to this morning's odor in the condo's elevator tainted by the scent of Doris's cigarette smoke and menthol cough drops. He felt his empty stomach give an upward lurch in response to the resurrected odor.

"Well, what does keep you there?" Matt punched the down button on the panel before them.

"I don't know… Location, comfort, routine. A couple of the old ladies are really nice. Every once in a while I come home to a pie by my front door or, or a container of homemade spaghetti."

"Any cougars amongst the residents?" Matt staged that boys' locker room bite to his lower lip, a bounce of his eyebrows.

Ash laughed as he stepped back to allow an office runner to exit the elevator, a bundle of manila envelopes engulfed in their arms. "Nope. And I'm not into necrophilia either." The door to the elevator closed with no other occupants within, and they began the glide downward to the first-floor cafeteria.

As Ash drove himself home that evening, he asked himself just why he continued to reside in the Old Folks Home, as Meredith referred to Parc LeMay, the three-story condominium building with its twelve units. The name was embossed on the front of the binder that held his minutes and receipts from the Home Owners Association. It was also on the letterhead of the quarterly newsletters and other pieces of official correspondence he sent out to the building's twelve residents. But it wasn't posted on the building façade or on the small grounds surrounding it. Maybe the building didn't merit having an identity, given its current state of decline.

The standalone condo building was in a good location, accessible to highways, a public park, hospitals and…and that was about it. There were no nearby entertainment venues, no trendy restaurants or stores. And there *was* Ms. Pitman just across the hall, always nosey, always snooping, and always bitterly critiquing Ash's every move.

Just what was keeping him there?

***

Ash picked up a ready-made fried chicken dinner from the deli of the nearby QuickieMart and headed for his building and the monotony of the Home Owners

Association meeting. The meetings had been conducted in exactly the same manner each month no matter who was president of the organization. They always began promptly at 6 p.m. with the Pledge of Allegiance, Ash holding the small American flag on a stick kept in the secretary/treasurer binder, and then followed by announcements.

The announcements focused on which resident (occasionally residents) was in the hospital, which residents were going to be visiting grandchildren out of town, thus mandating Operation Vigilant Neighbor be initiated, and which unit was going up for sale because the current resident was moving into a skilled care facility or was now residing in Mt. Olive Cemetery.

With the plastic wrap removed from the recyclable plate and the disposable fork and knife in hand, Ash picked at the cold green beans. He contemplated whether the foam tray itself could possibly have more flavor than its contents. He sat at the six-foot folding table in the condominium's lobby, sharing it with Vi Fabick, the current president of the HOA, and the vacant space for Jerry Kaplan, the current vice-president. All officers were listed as *current* because it wasn't unusual for offices to be vacated on short notice due to a fall, a heart attack, a stroke, even death due to natural causes...old age.

The meeting began with the customary unit by unit roll call conducted by Ash. He swallowed the tough piece of sinew from the scrawny chicken leg and scanned the scant attendance at the meeting. He found it disheartening to look at the frail figures seated in the metal folding chairs before him as he fought the distinct possibility he would be one of them in the future. He did a quick check of his teeth with his tongue and then began taking attendance:

"1A. Gwen Adams. Gwen?" called out Ash.

"Present."

"1B. Laverne Mueller. Laverne?"

"Here!"

"1C. Harry Hume. Harry? Harry?"

"He's in St. Luke's for tests," a voice replied.

"1D. May Clement. May? May Clement?"

"She's at her son's place in Toledo," another voice.

"2A. Jerry Kaplan. Jerry? Jerry told me he'd be in Austin this week," Ash recalled.

"2B. Judy King. Judy? Never mind. She called me this morning. Cold, flu, whatever."

"2C. Viola Fabick. Vi?"

"Of course I'm here. I'm the President."

"2D. Ralph McNeil. Ralph?"

"He's at the symphony tonight," a different voice.

"Harry? I thought you were in St. Luke's for tests. Who said Harry was in St. Luke's?" Ash scanned the gathered faces finding no one confessing their overreach. Trying to curb his irritation, he corrected the attendance record on his laptop. "Why didn't you say *you* were here Harry when I called your name? Jeez, Harry…" It was hard to be angry with Harry. He was probably the most congenial of all the building's residents, going out of his way to have a polite conversation and always concluding with a sincere compliment of some sort.

"And we can't just start voting on something we haven't discussed. The meeting hasn't even begun yet!" interjected a resident seated behind the artificial Ficus tree in a corner of the dreary lobby.

Ash pivoted in his metal folding chair to see who was hidden within the floral seclusion. "Gwen, can you come out of hiding so I can see who's speaking. And Harry, she's correct. We have to follow Roberts Rules; otherwise there's pandemonium." Ash recalled when pandemonium had ensued at prior HOA meetings, and it wasn't pretty.

The meeting was officially called to order, the minutes read, and the treasurer's report given. As Ash read his notes from the prior meeting, he took quick glances at the faces of the elderly residents. He felt a disheartening sensation, speculating they either didn't care or were just incapable of comprehending why multiple bids were necessary when looking for a service to seal the front driveway or to fix the foundation crack in the parking garage. But God forbid you would contract with a service without shopping around! Everyone knew of someone or had a brother-in-law in the business, and they would do the job for half the cost.

The floor was opened to the first and only item on the evening's agenda, that being the raising of the condo's assessment fee. Ash furiously attempted to record who said what in the heated debate that appeared to have only one side. No one, not one resident wanted to see an increase in the assessment no matter how noble its purpose. The consistent reason given was "being on a fixed income." There was only one resident to dissent. Ashton Walker.

"I hear your concerns, but look at this lobby," Ash began his counter argument, his law school education proving itself useful. He rose from his metal folding chair. "A $300 annual increase in the assessment can go towards updating this lobby. When was the last time it was remodeled? Look at the worn traffic pattern in the carpet from the front door to the elevator." If he'd had a staff in his hand, he could have parted the Dead Sea with the dramatic sweep of his arm. "Look at how dark and depressing it is with this paneling." He raised both of his hands emulating a preacher on a pulpit delivering hell fire and brimstone. Face it, courtrooms provide just as much theatrical entertainment as any musical on Broadway.

"It looks just fine to me." Doris Pitman. *Who else?*

"Ms. Pitman, it's the first impression a new buyer gets when they walk in the front door. You probably could easily get another $20,000 for your unit if this place had a facelift," was Ash's rebuttal. He sat backdown in his metal chair, certain he had made an indisputable point. After all, it takes money to make money.

"You mean my kids could get another twenty grand when I'm dead and gone," she huffed.

Ash collapsed his stature, now slouching in the cold metal folding chair. He realized even if he wanted to sell his unit, his profit margin was going to be stifled by the likes of Doris Pitman and the ten other tightwad senior citizens in his building *Why do I continue to live here amongst these geriatric downers and naysayers*, he wondered.

Ash entered the closing remarks of the meeting on his laptop and then shut it down. He took its slender silver case, the Parc LeMay binder, and his empty foam tray with the remnants of his dinner, now cold and inedible, into the nearby mailroom. He dropped his trash in the container just inside the small room that housed the twelve mailboxes with a shelf beneath to hold packages until collected by the residents. He heard the sound of Harry securing the door to the storage closet where the 6 ft. folding table and the twelve metal chairs were kept, Harry and Vi having worked together to put the furnishings of the lobby back in place.

Ash joined Vi Fabick, them being the last two people to remain in the condo's lobby. She had already pressed the UP arrow for the elevator and stood patiently waiting. She acknowledged Ash with a twisted smile, a look she often provided him and usually followed it with an off-color joke, totally inappropriate for the woman's advanced age. As a result, it made the risqué joke all the more hysterical and often bringing Ash to tears of laughter.

"I feel your pain, sweetie. I once was in your shoes, young and energetic, a true visionary." Vi met Ash in an open arm hug, surprising him with the strength of her tug. "And now I've become my mother, crotchety and penny pinching. If you're lucky, you'll be old someday too."

"No, I'll shoot myself before I'll ever let that happen."

Vi's face projected her shock at his statement but disintegrated into a broad grin, joining Ash in his own reverie. Ash sincerely enjoyed Vi's personality, finding they shared a mutual appreciation for dark humor, even bordering on the sadistic. His day always seemed a little brighter following an encounter with the bawdy woman.

"I didn't know Doris had kids." Ash said. "I thought she was an old maid, a…a spinster. Isn't that the term?"

"Doris *doesn't* have any kids. She has never even been married…not that that means anything these days. I don't know to whom she was referring tonight. She enjoy life..." Ash's voice reduced to a whisper, "And I can love her in return... I don't understand it... Why can't I find that someone, Vi?"

"Well, I sure as day don't understand it either, sweetie. If I were forty years younger, I'd be knocking on your door wearing only a smile. I guess I'll just have to settle with you sleeping a floor above me and not directly on me." The woman, younger at heart than her accrued years, released a giddy laugh and sauntered out of the elevator utilizing the exaggerated hip toss of a Las Vegas showgirl walking the runway, her raised hand giving a sweeping wave.

"Good night Vi." Ash smiled to himself, blushing slightly at the senior woman's flirtation as she continued her pompous strut towards her apartment.

Maybe if I were forty years older, he thought, smiling to himself.

***

Ash opened his unlocked front door, him feeling no need to lock up his apartment. He always felt safe and secure while in the building. If he left the building, then he locked his door. He knew his neighbors, and they kept a watch on each other and their property. You always let someone on your floor know if you were going to be gone for a couple of days so they wouldn't send the police looking for your body. If you were expecting a package, you had a neighbor pick it up, although no one had ever experienced a theft from the mailroom that Ash was aware of.

But the times were changing, and crime was encroaching into the area. There had been a recent string of car thefts two blocks over, reported on the evening news. And there had been the burglary of a dry cleaners he walked by when he'd need something from the QuickieMart on the next corner. He thought maybe he should start locking his door, even when he was home. Maybe it really was time to move.

Parc LeMay was three stories of condo units above a basement level parking garage for the residents' twelve cars. Not every resident owned a car, so some spaces usually remained vacant or were occasionally occupied by the vehicles of out-of-town guests. The garage was accessed via an asphalt driveway paved in the lower terrain behind the building, leading from a side street.

A black canvas canopy projected above the building's front door, reaching out to a horseshoe driveway. The asphalt pavement was bordered with manicured boxwood shrubs and a small grassy lawn giving the residential property a deceptively ritzy feeling. Once in the lobby, the perception was disproven, and the truth be told. The once high-class building was nothing more than a depressing home for the elderly these days.

The first two floors were covered in a façade of white brick and the third floor was surrounded in a faux copper mansard roof. There were small balconies projecting from the living room and equal size balconies off of the master bedroom of each unit. The tenants had a conglomeration of outdoor furniture and flower boxes on their personal outdoor space, each resident searching for their own identity in their choices.

Ash entered into his living room with a small dining room just off of the tiny kitchen. A hallway to his right led to the guest bedroom and bath and ended with the master suite with its larger bathroom and walk-in closet. The realtor had touted the apartment as being 1,212 square feet. Plenty of room for a bachelor when Ash, fresh out of law school, bought the place seven years ago.

Ashton Walker had graduated from the law school at Kansas City University and had passed the bar exam on his first attempt. He dazzled those who had interviewed him for his current position of Legal Counsel at PaseoParkTechnology, landing his first and only job as an attorney. They selected Ash over a candidate who had graduated from a flashier private university's School of Law. Ash occasionally wondered why? What had he brought to the table that the other guy hadn't?

On his first day on the job, Ash overheard the lady in human resources tell someone, "He's older than his years. He'll probably retire from here." He took the remark as a compliment, meaning he had maturity and stability. But he knew it was her candy-coated way of saying he was dull and predictable. He just hoped he would fit in with the people in his department. He wondered if the Big Bucks

University grad wouldn't have been a better fit, them being more social, a true extrovert, even flamboyant having come from an expensive school in a large city. It seemed everyone else with the firm projected dynamic personalities and verve, so much more than he did.

He had been with PaseoParkTechnology for almost eight years, and he did make good money. He had a 401k and profit sharing, three weeks of vacation annually, and an expense account he hardly ever used. He was invited to the weekly happy hours by his fellow attorneys and clerks but usually chose to depart immediately for his condo at the end of his Fridays. Now that he thought about it, those invitations had stopped a couple of years ago.

Ashton Walker wasn't a total recluse, but he wasn't a rousing party animal either. He considered Matt Blaylock, a fellow attorney at PaseoParkTechnology, to be his closest friend although they really didn't do anything socially outside of the office. They did meet for morning coffee before burying themselves in their offices, and they had lunch in the employee cafeteria if one of them wasn't on the road negotiating another merger. Ash held Matt in awe, admiring his unshakable self-confidence, at times appearing arrogant being so secure in his dealings. And Matt was one of those guys who commanded the eyes of women as he walked through the cafeteria. Those women didn't even notice Ash walking beside Matt. Their eyes always remained locked on Matt.

Chapter 3

Mascots and Mutts

"Well, it's unusual but not unheard of," Matt Blaylock said.

"If accounting can squeeze out another two million, then it should be a done deal," Ashton Walker put in his two cents.

The two attorneys for PaseoParkTechnology sat in Matt's office going over the play-by-play of a failed acquisition of a tech firm in Flagstaff, Arizona. Speculative opinions as to where the communication and the trust broke down were bantered about in the corner office. Ash was about to rise from his chair across from Matt's desk when a knock sounded on the doorframe and a feminine "ahem" interrupted his departure.

"Gentlemen, I would like you to meet Kristin Oakes. Kristin will be interning with us this semester." The lady from Human Resources turned to the stunning female standing to her left, "This is Matt Blaylock and...and..."

"Ashton, Ash Walker." Ash managed to rise to his feet utilizing the manners his grandmother had insisted upon. He felt his heart beating fast, trying to replace the blood that had drained from his head, and not because of his sudden movement. *Dang, she was beautiful!*

"I'm sorry. I knew your name was something odd." The woman from HR looked minimally embarrassed by her blunder.

Ash thought a better descriptor from the woman would have been, "Your name was unique, something unique." *Odd is the way you described the guy who still lives in his parents' basement.* At least Ash had his own place.

"Law student?" asked Matt, sitting upright and bringing his clasped hands to rest on his desktop, not even attempting to hide his lecherous ogling of the young lady.

"Yes. I'm in my second year at Wohlwend Hall. My hope is to join this company when I graduate in a couple of years. I'm taking a semester off and I figure interning will give me a bit of an edge." She matched Matt's lechery, a hint of her upper row of teeth tormenting her lower lip. The mating ritual was in play.

"Well, it's a good place to work. Nice perks and good people," Ash said. His deflating body descended back into his vacant chair. *No need to enter this competition,* he thought. *Matt already has this event marked as a W on his score card.*

"We'll let you gentlemen get back to your discussion." The woman from HR stepped back and with a swing of her arm gestured for the slender blonde to move onward to the next introduction.

Before the newbie turned to leave, she tilted her head ever so slightly. With unwavering confidence, she issued a dismissive, "Gentlemen." She included a subtle smile that would bring even God himself to His knees. Kristin Oakes turned and then placed one stiletto before the other, frictionlessly exiting Matt Blaylock's office. The swagger of her shapely hips was artfully executed as she followed the lady from HR through the sea of desks in the Legal Department.

"Wow...wow. Wohlwend Hall. What's their tuition now days? $80,000? $90,000 annually?" Ash asked once she was out of earshot.

He had already dismissed her as being out of his league. *No need to entertain the thought of a coffee date or a happy hour with the likes of her.* Not just because she attended Wohlwend Hall, but no one who looked like her would ever have any interest in him. He continued to watch through the open office door as the woman from HR introduce the nymph to the other faces in the Legal Department.

"Nepotism does have its perks." Matt rocked back in his desk chair, lacing his fingers behind his head. "Kristin Oakes..." He looked to see that Ash had not made the connection. "Oakes... Bernard Oakes, Chief Financial Officer's daughter."

"So, you wouldn't play that card if you had it in your hand? You wouldn't use a relative to move you into a coveted position and avoid waiting in line to get there?" baited Ash.

With that, Kristin Oakes looked back into Matt Blaylock's office from across the open floor, her eyes finding Ash's. Another one of those sensual smiles was gifted, this one meant only for him. He swallowed hard as his fingernails buried themselves into the arms of his chair. He tried to reciprocate but stopped, fearing his smile would appear more of a painful grimace, unable to match her in kind. *Had he ever seen anyone as gorgeous as her?*

"I've always said, "It's not who you know, it's who…you… blow." Matt rose from his desk to remove a legal guide from his bookcase. He glanced out his door to see the intern being directed to a waiting empty desk.

Ash, with a parting upward toss of his hazel eyes, returned to his own office. He resumed his day of reviewing documents, attempting to find precedence of a strategic move for rolling over 401ks in the process. He'd find himself occasionally replaying the interruption and the introduction in Matt's office this morning. He kept picturing Kristin Oakes in her heather gray dress, black stilettos, her silky ash blonde hair brushing her shoulders. And those eyes…gray- blue, making them mystical, alluring. *Dang, she was beyond gorgeous.*

What is it with women with money, that come from money? Ash wondered. *They always have that same aura.* It was an aura that continually took them out of Ash's reach. Ash dug a granola bar out of his bottom desk drawer. As he ate the dry grains in an attempt to curtail his growling stomach, he pondered what snacks someone like Kristin Oakes would keep in her bottom desk drawer. Did rich girls even eat power bars or snack on such junk? She'd probably never even eaten a granola bar in her entire sheltered life. Why was he even entertaining this, this

"Oh, yeah? What's their mascot?" Ash felt himself becoming a little less inhibited as the conversation took on a playful direction.

"You've never seen... Bollocks?"

"Bollocks? What?"

She moved closer to Ash, barely honoring the border of his personal space. "Bollocks . . . Peckers, Go-Nads, Dicks. Each sport at PCC has their own mascot and they're all bynames for male genitalia." Her eyes cascaded downwards and came to rest on the zipper of his suit pants. Not a trace of embarrassment encroached on her face, but Ash could feel his own cheeks starting to combust.

"Well...isn't that special," was his wilted retort, limp as his own genitalia had suddenly become.

She rocked up onto the toes of her $875 stilettos, pivoted, and seductively sauntered toward her waiting roadster. She called back over her shoulder, "See you tomorrow Ashton Walker."

There was indeed something to be said for Kristin Oakes's uninhibited spontaneity that had left Ashton Walker speechless, frozen in place on the employees' parking lot.

***

Ash drove through the drive thru at the Burger Palace he passed daily on his way to and from his office. Following his sexually charged conversation with the alluring intern he felt drained of the energy to cook this evening. He was truly speechless, even questioning if the exchange had really taken place. Was he reading too much into a perfectly innocent conversation? What if he had told her about college teams named the Titties, the Boobettes, the Jugs? Would that not constitute sexual harassment? Would he not be put on notice, perhaps even fired if he had shared those monikers and she chose to report him to Human Resources for doing so? But he'd never report her no matter who her father was...

He pulled his sedan into his assigned spot in the parking garage beneath the condominium building. The once dank and dark space now basked in a florescent glow of safety, the result of a HOA vote and an increase in assessments several years ago following the assault of a resident. A vagrant hiding in a corner of the garage had been discovered by Judy King coming home from her evening Bible study. Thankfully, Ralph McNeil was returning from dinner with his daughter and interrupted the attack. The perp was later apprehended by police in the park the next block over. Still, Ash exited his car and took a cautious gander of his surroundings, listening for any unusual noises.

He proceeded to the elevator, the door open and awaiting him. He took his double burger with mayo and lettuce only and the medium milkshake and fries out onto his living room balcony. He watched the white paper napkin with the restaurant's logo blow over the rail of the balcony and downward to the circle drive as he lost his grip on the wet container of the milkshake. He made a quick save, preventing the cold beverage from spilling onto the tabletop. He used his knee to move the chair from beneath the table, and he sat down to his dinner.

Was she coming on to him? Why him? Why not Matt? Had she already hit on Matt and he'd shut her down, not desperate to find a female in his bed? Matt had history. He probably even had a trophy case somewhere with trophies and medals celebrating his conquests and his victories, or at least a couple of pairs of lace panties to prove he had been where some men had never gone before. What did Ashton Walker have? He had his virginity, that's what he had. That night with Allison Boyd didn't count. Neither did the night with Maddie Allen. A night with Kristin Oakes would most definitely count . . . Like that would ever happen.

Ash finished his fast-food feast, threw his trash into the can in the corner of his kitchen. It was then he realized that he hadn't retrieved today's mail from his mailbox in the building's lobby. He opened the door to his unit, not even caring if Doris Pitman was standing butt naked in front of her own door. He could use a good laugh tonight. Yeah, it was going to be one of those nights, wasn't it?

Tonight, he just wanted to talk to someone, to anyone. He was tired of his own voice, tired of the redundant stories he told in his own lonely head. He longed for a physical connection to a fellow human being. Usually during times like these, he would give his sister a call. But lately she had been consumed with her own kids, running them to baseball practice or dance lessons. Often his calls would go directly to her voicemail, and they might not be returned for a day, even longer. And it wasn't her job to fill the void in his life. *That would border on incest.*

He rode the vacant elevator to the first floor, smelling an unidentified odor. Harry Hume's cigar? A grandkid's full diaper? A rotten egg found in someone's refrigerator? He took an immediate deep breath of fresh air when the door opened. He crossed the worn-out orange and red carpet, stepping onto the dingy tile floor of the mailroom. Tonight he noticed the worn pattern of shoe soles in the linoleum flooring, residents having stood in the same couple of spots while skimming through a handful of letters and bills. *Was the tile seriously that old or was it just cheap quality to begin with?*

He saw a few packages on the shelf noting deliveries of medications, evidenced by their return labels for pharmaceutical firms advertised on television during the evening news. He wondered just how many of those little yellow prescription bottles were in the condo building at any one time. What was the average number per apartment? Was there a direct ratio to the age of the resident, the older they were the more prescriptions filled? How soon would there be packages addressed to him? What would his ailment, or ailments, be? ...Probably erectile dysfunction, and not from over use.

"I know what you mean about a change of scenery. It does get old around here sometimes." He said words intended for her but directed more so at the depressing décor of the lobby. *The place doesn't look much better in the dark,* he thought. *You just can't see the age and wear as well as you can in daylight.*

"Especially in winter. I hate winter. Winter's coming." She brought her fist to her mouth stifling a quiver of her chin. Ash wondered if the palsy was caused by either her advanced age or her state of mind, but perhaps more so a little of both.

"You're right there. I get S-A-D. Do you get S-A-D?" he asked.

"S-A-D? What's that?"

"Seasonal Affective Disorder. It's a feeling of depression that comes from a lack of sunshine and vitamin D."

"How do you know about that? You a doctor?"

"No," he laughed, "A lawyer."

"Nothing wrong with that unless you like to chase ambulances."

"No, I'm corporate. I chase companies."

The two lonely people found themselves just sitting in the silence of the lobby, but it wasn't a bad thing. They were sitting together. They were listening to each other's breathing, smelling the same air freshener from the plug-in hidden by the fake Ficus, watching the same moon rising through the lobby's picture window. They weren't alone; they weren't by themselves.

Ash looked out the window to see the movement of a raccoon crossing the horseshoe driveway and heading for the open drainage sewer, but he didn't bother to tell Mrs. King. He knew the critter would be long gone before she could locate it. He just went back to thinking his own depressing thoughts.

She broke the silence. "I wish I had a dog. We always had a dog before my husband died. They were such good company, never demanding, never mean…" She released a small cackle as she savored a personal memory.

"I'm allergic to dogs, but I do enjoy watching them. They can be characters."

"We had corgis. They liked to sleep on their backs and do the zoomies!" She released a reflective laugh, a smile remaining behind.

"Aren't those the kind of dogs the Queen of England had?"

"Yeah." A sad smile over took the elderly woman's face. "I don't think she had any towards the end, either."

"I heard her son, Prince Andrew, took them in." Ash sat up straight, a stellar thought coming to mind. "Why don't you get a small dog?"

"You know we can't have dogs here! You're, you're on the Home Owner's Association board. You of all people should know the rules." Ash was the recipient of a hardnose glare.

"But if you have a doctor's script, you can have a support dog. It's ADA approved."

"You sure about that?" Ash could see the lights coming on in the woman's eyes behind her heavy-rimmed glasses.

"Absolutely! I'm an ambulance chaser! Remember?" He included a genuine smile to solidify his position.

"Oh, honey! I...I don't know if I could even take good care of a dog anymore."

"Well, it's a thought. It would give you some company and even get you some exercise walking it."

"I could use that!" Her lower lip protruded.

"Well, Mrs. King, you have a good evening. I've got to go and run a load of laundry or I'm going commando to work tomorrow."

"What do you mean, *commando*?"

"Without any underwear."

"Go do your laundry, son."

Ash just went with his impulse. He leaned over and put a gentle kiss on the top of the elderly woman's head, smelling talcum powder and a hint of lavender scented soap. It brought back memories of his own long-departed grandmother who had raised him.

Ash attempted to appear suave and debonair, walking casually down the open aisle of the sixth floor towards his office. Wanting to search for the intern he kept his eyes directed forward, attempting to appear disinterested. He entered and hung his suitcoat on the hook stuck to the glass of the door. As he moved towards his desk, he took a leisurely glance into the open center of law clerks and administrative assistants in the Legal Department. He searched for where the intern had landed. He thought he saw her just as he rounded his desk, a support pillar now taking her out of his line of sight.

He went through the motions of shuffling papers, skimming briefs, and initialing on the highlighted line on documents. After about an hour of performing the charade he grabbed a random piece of paper from his desktop and headed for the department's copy machine. He waited patiently behind a senior litigator, nodding at her apology for taking so long. Standing there, he glanced in the direction of the new intern's desk only to find the desk's chair empty. Where was she?

"So, are you going to Glenda's retirement party?" It was her voice. He could already recall and recognize her voice.

He spun to see her standing directly behind him, again testing the parameters of his personal space. "Glenda? Who's Glenda?"

"The woman whose retirement party invitation is in your hand." She smoothly nodded towards the piece of paper he had snatched from his desktop.

Ashton Walker looked down at the hot pink piece of stationery with its border of colorful pansies grasped in his hand, "Join us in saying farewell to Glenda" across the top of the page. He felt an immediate bombardment of butterflies in his stomach. "Oh! This Glenda. Yeah, I'm, I'm thinking about going. You?" *Why would Kristin Oakes go to someone's retirement party when she has only worked here for two days? She probably hadn't even met Glenda yet. I can't even recall who the heck Glenda is!*

"I always enjoy a good party." The young woman's sensual smile again seized his psyche, her eyes demanding his.

"Maybe I'll see you there." He wondered if his genitals could retract any more.

"Here. I'm finished," stated the senior litigator with her arms full of copied documents. She turned and did a little bob and weave, trying to pass between Ash and the intern.

"Thank you." Ash tried to regain his composure as he placed the hot pink paper under the copier's flap.

"You might want to turn it print side down," smoothly suggested the intern.

"Yeah…yeah."

Ash spun to face the beautiful woman dead-on. He bent forward, planting his palms on his thighs and released a riotous laugh. "I'm going to break every bone in his body! I'm going to rip out his eyes and every tooth in his big dumb mouth!"

"From whose big mouth? From Bernard Oakes's mouth?" She was striking a sultry pose, one hand on her hip, the other behind her neck and flipping her smooth braid.

"No…no. Blaylock, Matt Blaylock. He walked me straight into this one."

"I don't give a damn who walked you where!" She reclaimed Ash's bicep with both of her hands. "I just want you to walk me to the nearest bar and then home."

Ash felt a rush of relief cascade over his being. The playing field had been leveled, her stature reduced to much the same as his. Both fatherless, both reared in marginalized homes. He felt his apprehension dissipating and a building of his self-confidence that he truly was deserving of a woman like Kristin Oakes.

There was that activity in his boxers again, and this time it wasn't limp.

***

"Jerk," Ash huffed.

"Who me?" Matt looked up from the *Pinnacles in Business* magazine open on his desk.

"Well who else am I staring at, at this exact moment? Bernard Oakes's daughter, my ass. He's not her father. *And*, she's a Wohlwend Hall legacy, and she's about to flunk out." Ash leveled his best *so there!* glare on Matt. He took his usual chair before Matt's cluttered desk.

"How did you find all of this out?" Matt got up from his desk and closed the glass door to his office. He sprinted back to his waiting desk chair and gave his full attention to Ash in anticipation of a notably hot piece of gossip.

"We went to Trailblazer's for a drink after work yesterday. The drunker she got, the more I found out about her. I called her an Uber after about an hour, and I drove myself home. Last thing I need is to get fired because the flakey ditz tells HR a bunch of lies. I don't know what I was thinking!"

"Oh man…" Matt was searching his brain for which question to ask first. "So tell me what happened."

"It was like…like she… Let's just say there are girls in middle schools who are more mature than her."

"So what… so how… tell me how you ended up with her at Trailblazers."

Ash provided Matt with a play-by-play of the encounter at the copier. He told him about the reveal of her pedigree, Bernard Oakes NOT being her father. And he went on to tell of sexual advances and blatant innuendos from the attractive young lady over a couple of beers at the nearby bar.

acknowledging nod of her head. *She didn't see it as a match made in heaven. Perhaps they were too far on opposite ends of the spectrum.*

Having failed to get Kristen Oakes's phone number, he wondered how he would ever speak to her again. He added the garnering of her phone number to his to-do list for tomorrow, slipping Bernice her favorite candy bar in exchange for the piece of confidential information. And he again fought the feelings that he really wasn't her type, and he wasn't so sure that she was his type. He had no use for women who were deceptive, flighty and high maintenance like Krissy Oakes. At least he tried to tell himself that.

"I have a housekeeper who needs a trial this coming Saturday. Can I send her to your place?" Meredith inquired over her glass of wine.

"Yeah, the place is kind of dusty and the sink can't hold any more dirty dishes."

"You're pathetic," she laughed. Meredith became noticeably quiet, hedging if she wanted to share her thoughts. "This one's kind of...different. I can't put my finger on it, but I just feel there's more than she's willing to tell."

"I just serve as your testing ground. I don't ask questions and I don't judge. I leave that for Doris." Ash realized he hadn't seen his neighbor, Doris Pitman, in at least a week. *Is that a new record? Maybe I should go sniff around her unit's door when I get home this evening to see if her corpse is rotting within.*

"Well anyway, her name is Corinne, and she should be at your place at 9 a.m. Oh! Brenda, the lady who was cleaning your condo's lobby, moved to St. Louis, so I'm looking for a replacement."

"I figured as much. I emptied the trash can from the mail room. It was overflowing."

With dinner finished, Ash played a video game with his nephew and read a bedtime story to his niece. The youngsters were off to bed by 8 p.m., and Ash sat down with his sister at the dining room table to share a second slice of tiramisu with a cup of decaf. It was during times like this that their sibling bond kicked into overdrive.

Meredith delivered her look, the one signifying a serious discussion was on the horizon. "Ash, do you think you'll ever find someone to settle down with?"

"I don't know. If it's meant to be, it will be. I'm…I'm good on my own."

"You may be good, but will you ever be great?"

"Look at you since Dale died. Are you great? Are you even good?"

Meredith took another fork full of tiramisu. "I'm on a different playing field than you are. I don't have time to date and play silly relationship games. Usually once I say, 'I have two children,' the guy is dropping a twenty on the bar and heading for the door."

"Sad." Ash shook his head at his sister's consistent misfortune.

barely a thud as the lock reset itself. He then almost tiptoed down the hallway to his front door.

Sheeeeew. Missed me!

***

Promptly at 9 a.m. on Saturday morning, Ash heard a knock on his front door. He looked through the small peep hole to see a woman who didn't fit the profile of housekeepers his sister consistently hired. He recalled that he had been warned, Meredith stating that this one didn't *fit the mold.*

The woman standing before the closed door looked uncomfortable to the point of being on the verge of tears. She was older than the prior candidates for a custodial career by easily twenty, maybe even thirty years. As a matter of fact, she looked like she should be knocking on the door of the Social Security Office and not the condominium of Ashton Walker.

Ash saw behind the woman, the door of Doris Pitman's unit open. Today, Doris was wearing a housecoat in a madras plaid of pastel colors. The pink sponge curlers were once again adhering to her head and corralled by a heavy black hairnet. She immediately began studying the backside of his visitor. Ash snatched open his door in an attempt to spare the candidate from having to interact with Doris. But he was too late to prevent the confrontation.

"Are you selling something? Solicitors are *not* allowed in this building," snapped Doris. "There's a sign right on the front door to the lobby."

"Doris, she is coming to see me," Ash said. He rationalized Doris was probably just as caught off guard as he was with the woman's appearance and advanced age in comparison to all the other job applicants.

"Well... have a nice day." And Doris disappeared back into her unit.

"I'm sorry," Ash said, looking at the woman's brittle face. "Doris is the self-proclaimed mayor of the building. We just let her have her delusions of grandeur." The visitor actually allowed a slight smile to appear on her face, appearing a little relieved at the reduced formality of the situation. "Please, come in." He stood back to permit her entry into his living room.

She stood just inside the doorway. The yellow plastic bucket with the logo for The Cleaning Contessa dangled from her hand. It contained cleaning solutions in spray bottles and a variety of sponges. Her eyes roamed the open living/dining room combination and spent a little more time looking into the unobstructed opening of the kitchen.

"I'm Ash, Meredith's brother. I guess she already told you that and how this trial works."

"Yes, yes she did." The woman lowered the bucket to his hardwood floor and moved curiously through the living room, her head oscillating to look at the

"We…we was in foster care. We, we all got split up eventually…"

"Oh, I see--"

"I don't want to talk about it no more… I've got work to do."

"I understand. But please feel free to take the monkey…if you'd like it."

She turned her back to him, he thought to perhaps hide her tears. "No, no. It's yours now." And she resumed efficiently dusting his living room, carefully moving and replacing other items bought in other antique stores and flea markets. Ashton Walker wondered if any of the other dustables, as he referred to the trinkets, sparked other memories for the woman, those too eliciting obvious pain and sorrow.

***

"So how did she do?" Meredith asked on the other end of Ash's cell phone.

"Fine. Good, really good." He tried to sound sincerely enthusiastic in his rating of Corinne. She had done a good job. His condo unit was once again clean and waiting for guests…who never came to his place.

"If you're really satisfied with her work, I'm thinking of assigning her to your building, to replace the woman who moved to St. Louis."

"Yeah, you can give her a try here. And, be warned, the lobby is becoming a trash pit."

Ash had found himself perseverating on his mental image of and his interaction with the cleaning woman even with her departure from his condo being five hours ago. He had replayed the incident with the toy monkey over and over in his head. The woman's internal pain was pervasive for the remainder of her time in his apartment, Ash feeling it too.

"What's her story anyway? When compared to your other candidates, she is totally out of character."

"I know, right? She was referred to me by a neighbor. She said Corinne just showed up at her church one Sunday, sat in her pew and started singing the hymn. Debbie said the woman has a voice like…like who was that woman on that talent show a few years ago? Oh, you know who I'm talking about! It was totally unexpected!"

"Wow!" With the phone tucked beneath his chin, Ash reached for a beer in his clean, but reorganized refrigerator. The few bottles of beer were shoved to the back of the appliance, hidden behind the pitchers that he kept iced tea and orange juice in. He moved several items, returning them to his preferred order.

"She's kind of a charity case from what I've been told. Domestic abuse victim, kids taken by family services, occasionally homeless, the whole nine yards. I don't know how true the story is or if it's just speculation on the part of my friend, but Corrine obviously has not had an easy life."

Ash didn't know why but his mouth did that thing again, not totally engaging his brain and not waiting for his permission to open and spew. But the words just flowed out.

"Can you get someone else to be your test site and schedule Corinne to clean my place once a week? Nothing extensive. Maybe bathrooms and kitchen every week, and then the entire place the opposite week? It'd probably take her what, two, three hours max? And since she's in the building, she can do the lobby and hallways, saving her a second trip."

"Really? Why would you want her to do that? I'd think the redhead from a few months ago would be more your speed. She even told me to let her know if you ever decided to have a regular cleaning person. I think she liked you."

"Redhead?" Ash searched his memory. "Oh yeah. I remember that one. I was missing one of my favorite pairs of boxer shorts after she left. I think she took them as a souvenir."

"You never told me this!" Meredith managed between hiccups of laughter. "Did you two—"

"No, we didn't, although she would have liked to. I'm not accustomed to your housekeepers consistently dropping innuendos and then dropping pieces of their clothing to the floor as they clean."

"She didn't! She really was cute, but she was as dumb as a box of rocks…"

Chapter 6

When Will it be My Turn?

He pulled the door open to the mom-and-pop Italian restaurant allowing an elderly couple to exit first. He wondered if everyone dining at Vito's Trattoria received the senior discount, that is, everyone except for him. Vito himself saw the somewhat regular customer enter, Ash now standing by the hostess' podium.

"Pisano! Long time, no see!"

"Hey, Vito. Yeah, it's been a while. It's good to be back."

"You wanna sit in-a booth or a table?"

"A booth is fine." Ash felt self-conscious eating alone, although he had done just that almost his entire life of thirty-two years. There were those few occasions when he'd bring Meredith with him, and a couple of times a date. But the vast majority of times it was just him and his desire for that elusive companion to share his life with.

He ordered his usual glass of red wine and an appetizer of mussels marinara, followed by his customary spaghetti Bolognese. As he sat waiting for the first course, he brought his cell phone from his pants pocket. He felt that staring at the screen saver on his phone served the purpose of making him look like he was not alone. He had friends. They just weren't with him this evening.

He brought up his email to find a couple of advertisements and an unopened email from PaseoParkTechnology. He clicked on the subject line to open an email from the Head of Legal.

Ashton, a small firm in Seattle, Washington is having a difficult time comprehending how a merger works. I need you to fly to Seattle this Wednesday and spend Thursday and Friday explaining it to their lawyer. Bernice will make your travel arrangements in the morning. Stop by her desk when you arrive and work out any details. You should be able to spend the weekend in Seattle getting a little R & R, and then return on Sunday afternoon/evening. Feel free to take Monday morning as comp time for your extended hours.

Business travel wasn't common for Ash, but it wasn't unusual either. As the two bachelors in the Legal Department, either Ash or Matt were typically assigned the trips. Ash supposed that his name was up on the roster for this trek to Seattle. He really didn't mind. It broke the monotony, and it provided him with an opportunity to scout other jobs in other regions of the country should he ever leave PaseoParkTechnology. But he knew that was never going to happen if he had any control over the matter.

Sitting in the booth, he could feel his mood steadily turning glum. He sipped his wine and tried to savor the spaghetti while he watched two couples on a double date being seated at a table in his line of sight. He'd take quick glances at the exchanges, verbal and nonverbal, between the males and the females. He felt his appetite wane as he watched the tactile exchanges of tender squeezes and hands resting on bare arms. He watched quick kisses and lingering smiles. *Those types of moments don't occur between a person and their cell phone,* he thought wistfully. *I can't even fake those sensations and feelings.*

He flagged the waitress over, requested a to-go box and his check. He walked languidly back to his condo, consumed by a sense of longing. He hardly noticed the drop in temperature and the beginning drops of rain, the changes merely supporting his dour mood.

There but for the grace of God go I, he thought. *When is God going to direct me to someone or someone to me?*

***

Bernice, the administrative assistant to the Head of Legal, found Ash a flight from Kansas City to Seattle by way of St. Louis. There were seldom if ever any direct flights to any of the cities he was sent to. But at least the company had no problem putting him in First Class, and they also booked him in pricy boutique hotels near five-star restaurants. And they never blinked an eye at his expense reports, submitted upon his return to Kansas City. Then again, Ash wasn't an extravagant person, often skipping breakfast or an occasional lunch. His dinners dependent on how willing he was to relinquish the lifestyle he had become accustomed to. Ash thought to himself *I, personally, would like to at least give it a try.*

Again, Ash felt his phone vibrate in his pocket. He stood from the high-top bar table, removed the phone, and again he saw the same unknown number on the caller ID. He also saw a voice mail message had been left with the first call. He excused himself from the depressing celebration and stood in the quiet of the hallway by the men's room of the tavern to listen to the message. He pressed the voice mail icon and listened to her voice:

"Ash, it's Krissy. Uncle Bernie got your phone number for me from HR. I hope you don't mind. I was wondering if you'd like to meet at Trailblazer's for a drink tonight. I promise not to make as big a fool of myself as I did the last time. Call me…please."

What time is it here in Seattle? What time is it in Kansas City? Why do I even care? Why? Because I like Krissy Oakes. As ditzy as she is, she is still gorgeous. And most importantly, she obviously likes me. She sought me out. Maybe she actually wants me!

Chapter 7

A Long Flight Home

Ashton Walker calculated the time change. It was 12:20 p.m. in Seattle, Washington, making it 2:20 p.m. in Kansas City. She had just called him, so obviously it wasn't too early or too late for him to return her call. He went to his list of recent calls, resting his index finger on the last call with its odd area code. His phone began to dial the ten digits, and as he held the phone to his ear he could feel his heart palpitating a little faster, a little stronger.

"Hello Ashton Walker," she answered.

"Well hello Krissy Oakes. How's your uncle?" he teased.

"Bernie is well... He wanted to know why I needed the phone number for one of his company's lawyers. I told him I had just gotten the results of a paternity test from my doctor, and I needed to share the good news with you." She released a laugh causing Ash to feel a hint of activity below the waist. Even her laugh was adorable.

"Great. I guess we'll be the topic of the lunchroom at PaseoParkTechnology."

"No, I just told him I borrowed $10 bucks from you, and I wanted to pay you back. So, not only do I have your phone number, but I now have your address, your social security number and your emergency contact information."

for hitting on the niece of the CFO if she no longer worked at PaseoParkTechnology? Is there some statute of limitations in place? What about a noncompete clause of some sort?

Ash appreciated the interior of the sports car, his hand feeling the polished woodgrain of the dashboard. He looked through the steering wheel to ascertain the purpose of the numerous dials and gauges, checking the speedometer to see Krissy was only doing seven miles above the speed limit. Not enough to draw the attention of a cop unless they wanted to harass the car's owner, letting their own jealousy override their professionalism.

"So how did your discussion go with Uncle Bernie when you told him you no longer wanted to attend Wohlwend Hall or be a lawyer for PaseoParkTechnology?" he asked warily. "You did have the conversation, didn't you?"

She released an uninhibited snort. "He told me he didn't want to work at PaseoParkTechnology anymore, either. All of my fear and apprehension was for naught."

"Good. Good. I'm relieved for you."

The German sports car pulled into a vacant space on the parking lot for Trailblazer's Tavern. The couple got out of the sleek little car, meeting up in front of the car just as the vehicle's headlights chose to dim, then turn off. Ashton

Walker summoned every ounce of sophistication and charm residing in his body and pulled Krissy Oakes into his arms, placing a kiss on her lips.

He had rehearsed this moment multiple times in his head, beginning with the pilot's welcome aboard announcement this morning and ending with the smooth touchdown of the 737 on the tarmac of KCI this evening. In a self-evaluation, he felt he had mastered the technique. His performance had been impeccable. Although greatly over planned, he believed it had truly come off as being spontaneous.

"You know," she said, stepping back to look into his eyes. She took the lapels of his jacket into her clenched hands, pulling herself back into his chest then tilting her head back to give him her full attention. "I'm really not all that thirsty. I'm more...hungry. I think I'd like to see what you have in your refrigerator."

"Seriously?" he scoffed, again fearing the cracking voice of his adolescent version. *Was this a little too soon in our relationship? Perhaps. But isn't this exactly what he had hoped for, longed for? Even prayed for?*

"I never enjoy sex on an empty stomach." Her lips were on his again.

He now had his answer. *Yeah, she wants me too.*

***

She pulled the sleek vehicle to the curb of the horseshoe driveway before his condo building. Ash reflected that the only time cars were parked there overnight was when the daughters of the elderly residents spent the night watching over their ill parents. And the daughters' cars were usually minivans or well-worn SUVs, not flashy imported sports cars. He predicted the gossip hotline of the building would be a buzz beginning at 5 a.m. if things indeed went as he hoped. It would be 5 a.m. when Mrs. King of Unit 2B would peer over her bedroom's balcony to check the morning's weather. And there she would see Krissy's car, a thin layer of frost on the tinted windshield, the telltale sign of being parked there all night.

Within minutes, the residents of Parc LeMay would be playing a live version of *Clue*, trying to solve who had a visitor, the purpose of their visit, and why they had stayed all through the night. Replace the candlestick, lead pipe, revolver, rope, wrench and knife with a sleek black imported roadster, and the victim would most likely reside in Unit 3C and not the library, billiard room or the conservatory. Ashton Walker's face would be on the playing card in the hand of the winner.

He cringed as he opened the door into the noxiously garish lobby, Krissy following closely behind him. Ash tried to remain neutral in his reaction, hoping the woman in his company wouldn't notice the odor of Gwen Adams' overpowering perfume mixing with the smell of the sauerkraut and smoke sausage May Clement had made for her dinner that evening. It was all he could do to stifle his own gag reflex. Ash tipped his chin towards the elevator cattycorner to the

"I know that." She playfully nudge him with her shoulder, signifying her acceptance of his single ground rule.

As the doors opened onto the third floor, Ash's chest was gripped with terror. It was still evening, with a tad of daylight outside. The third-floor security guard was probably still awake, still on duty. Would Doris hear the hum of the motor, the movement of the elevator's door? Who was he kidding? She always did! He braced himself for the inevitable.

With his garment bag over his arm and the handle of his carry-on in the same hand, he took the beauty's upper arm with his free hand and attempted to guide her to his apartment, hoping to significantly increase the speed of their forward motion. He fumbled in his pants pocket to locate his door key, fending off loose change and a few candy mints he had picked up from a bowl on a hostess's station at breakfast that morning. He stood poised at his door, the key placed in the lock, just in time to hear the door of Unit 3D being pulled open into Doris Pitman's apartment.

Ashton Walker froze as he saw the frumpish body of Doris Pitman in his peripheral vision, standing in her open doorway. She looked like a matronly mannequin in the plus size section of a women's clothing store. She was wearing loud pink pastel pants and a flower covered blouse, probably selected straight from the clearance rack at the local discount store. Even her makeup could only be described as clown-like in its unnatural shades of red lipstick and apricot blush. *Is that turquoise eye shadow?*

"Ashton."

"Ms. Pitman."

Doris studied the couple for only a matter of seconds through her narrowed eyes and then stepped back into her apartment, closing the door behind her.

Ash knew an inquisition awaited him in the not-so-distant future, and it would culminate with a cheap shot taken by the fractious old woman at his speculatory behavior this evening. He surmised she was already in the process of composing her scathing soliloquy as Ash pushed his front door open and flipped the light switch to illuminate his living room. But then he felt a self-congratulatory smile overtaking his face.

Hopefully Doris would be spot on this time. Hopefully her tongue lashing would be pinpoint accurate and well deserved. He would not only welcome her scalding words but would appreciate them, as he wore his deed like a badge of honor. This time he would find delight in her verbal assault, not even attempting to deny it. And he would thank her profusely for her spot-on assessment of his lurid behavior, thus baffling the living daylights out of the old biddy. *Bring it on Doris!*

Krissy Oakes followed Ash into his apartment. He dropped his carry-on bag to the floor and draped his garment bag over the back of a chair in his living room.

He surveyed the room, trying to see it as she was seeing it for the first time. Receiving her positive opinion of his living quarters would serve as all the more confirmation that he was indeed worthy of a woman like her.

"Well, this is my home."

"I like it...." She voiced her sincere approval, her hand sliding over the back of the matching chair to the chair now holding his garment bag. She glided towards the French door to the balcony and looked out to see the tops of the bare trees. "Your neighbor across the hall seems like a real witch."

"Doris? Yeah, she's the deluxe version. She's just a very unhappy person and likes to share her misery with everyone. Care for a glass of wine?"

Ash had remembered a bottle of White Zinfandel was tucked in the back of his refrigerator, a gift from Esther Price, Unit 3B, from two Christmases ago. He guessed it was still good, but most likely a low-end brand from a grocer's and not a genuine store for wines. It would just have to do for this occasion, the alcohol serving to relax the two candidates for the evening's acts of debauchery in Unit 3C.

He opened the refrigerator door, pleasantly surprised to find another bottle of wine, a quality vintage he had enjoyed on previous occasions when having dinner at his sister's house. It was located front and centered on the same shelf as the cheap wine. One of Meredith's calling cards had been left beside it. Ash turned the card over to read: *Thank you for choosing The Cleaning Contessa. Please call* the chosen disc. She dropped it in and pushed the button to make the disc disappear, causing the music to play. The music softly filled his living room.

He was caught off guard by her choice. "Glenn Miller? Really? That CD belonged to my dad."

"Moonlight Serenade, the penultimate dance piece." She raised her arms as she began to sway to the music. "Come. Dance with me."

Ashton Walker obliged, taking Kristin Oakes into his aching arms. He felt the surge of boiling lust in his veins, tempered with the combined joy of his dream coming true and a fear of his hopes being dashed by a sudden wrong move on his part. As they swayed as one he had to know, he had to ask.

"If this is the penultimate dance piece, what is the ultimate dance piece?"

"Whatever my husband and I choose for our first dance at our wedding reception."

What a perfect answer, what a spotless response! What would Kristin Oakes and I choose?

As the melody came to an end, he led her back to his sofa. They took their glasses of wine from the low industrial cart, taking a sip to somewhat quench the intensity of feelings arcing between them. He smoothly brought his mouth to hers, once again as he had mentally rehearsed on his flights home. She slithered beneath his waiting arm with her lips meeting his, her fingers skillfully unbuckling the belt of his suit pants.

And with that, the grand opening ribbon was cut on the festivities in Unit 3C.

"Oh . . . oh." *Was he disappointed?* "Yeah, perhaps you are on to something. Maybe with some time."

Had he already arrived at the designated destination of Love? *Wait! Where was the always cautious, always level headed Ashton Walker? What happened to that guy? Was spontaneity a communicable disorder, him not being vaccinated to prevent such occurrences of unplanned events and opportunities. Was there such a thing as "too soon"?...Was it too soon to pick the music for their first dance?*

Following breakfast, Ash left Krissy at the driver's door of her sporty ride. A quick kiss was shared, and then he took a couple of steps back as the car's six-cylinder twin turbo engine roared out of the horseshoe driveway. He reentered his building, deciding to take the fire escape to the third floor, thus postponing the pending inquisition by Doris Pitman as much as he was looking forward to sharing his defining indiscretion with the old biddy.

***

As Ash reentered the three-story building, the elevator doors opened, and he heard the yipping barks of a small dog. A scruffy mongrel tethered to a red leather leash pulled towards him through the parted door. He followed the leash to the walker of Judy King, who was attempting to keep up with the yapping ball of fur.

"Well, that didn't take you very long!" He reached down to allow the spastic pup to sniff his extended hand.

"Oh, Ash! My daughter took me Friday to the shelter. Meet Emmitt King."

"Welcome to the neighborhood Emmitt!" He threw his concerns of an allergy attack to the wind and went in for a tussle with the playful pup.

"He's an older dog, but he still has a lot of spunk. He's housebroke, and he's a snuggler."

"He sounds like a perfect match for you."

"And Ralph and Laverne are going to talk to their doctors about writing a letter so they can get a companion too."

Ash reeled with the possibility he may have unwittingly started a trend in Parc LeMay. How would his allergy respond to a building full of dogs and cats? But Mrs. King sure looked happy for a change. What was an occasional hive or two if it made someone else happy?

He entered his apartment to the ringtone of his cell phone. He followed its marimba sound to his coffee table, exactly where he had left his phone last night as the fireworks began to unfold between Krissy and him. He answered the call from Meredith on the final ring.

"Hey, Mer—"

"So who is she? Will I approve?"

"She's a young lady who interned at PaseoParkTechnology for three days and then dropped out of law school. Didn't I tell you about her already?" He his office, his bare feet feeling the coolness of the hardwood floor. He saw the back of Corinne Collins as she rewound the toy monkey taken from his coffee table and carefully cradled it in her hands as it played the tiny cymbals.

"Take it." She jumped at the sound of his voice. "I insist. It means so much more to you than it ever will to me. It's yours."

"Th...thank you." She kept her eyes diverted.

"Do you have other siblings? Other family still in Camdenton?" Ash sat on the arm of one of his living room chairs watching the woman caress the little monkey, tracing its features with her finger.

"I did. They...they ended up in other homes, too... Within a few years we all lost track of each other. An' Family Services in the country that many years ago, they weren't too concerned with keeping six kids together. They was doing good to just find homes fer even one or two of us kids."

"I see. Have you ever tried to find your family?"

"Nah, that all cost money." She got a sheepish grin on her face as she brought her face up to look into his hazel eyes, "Lawyers is expensive."

"Lawyers! Those lowlife scoundrels!" he teased back. "Do you know your siblings' full names? Dates of birth? Place of birth? Your parents' names? Anything pertinent that could be used to identify a connection with you?"

"I was pretty young the last time I saw any of them, probably about nine, maybe ten years old. I'd need to sit down and really try to conjure up some memories."

"Do it. Do it this week. Make a list to the best of your knowledge of just that, names, dates, locations. I'll see what I can do."

Corrine warily looked at the man, "How much would you charge?"

"I'd do it pro bono publico." He saw the blank look on her face. "I'd do it for free, in my spare time."

Her face revealed her distrust. "Now why would you go and do that? Why would you do that fer me?"

"I have the feeling you are a good person, and you would do the same for me if you had the ability to do so."

"You and yer sister . . . Youse both good people."

"Hey, we are all in this life together. Think how much more pleasant things would be if we did what we could for each other without expecting anything in return."

She started to push the dust mop across the living room's floor, but hesitated. She covered the top of the broomstick with both her hands and then rested her chin on top of them. A cunning grin began to give rise exposing the conducted within the statutes of limitations...wasn't it? He mustered his courage and rose from his desk. He stepped around to meet the man, extending his right hand forward.

"It's a pleasure to meet you, sir." The man appeared much younger than Ash had envisioned, thus making the meeting even more startling. *A CFO of a 500 Level company and maybe only fifty years old?*

"I decided to see who has my niece's attention these days."

"Well, she certainly has mine. Won't you have a seat?"

In all sincerity, Ash wished a trapdoor would open in the floor and the man would drop from his sight. Bernard Oakes was intimidating not only with his size and structure, but his attitude was coming through loud and clear. Ash didn't enjoy having someone else's eyes bore so forcefully into his own. It was unnerving.

"No, thank you. I have some pressing things to deal with as I'm sure you do too, so I won't keep you from it." The formidable man straightened his shoulders even broader and added another inch or two to his already impressive height. "Let me just say that my niece is my pride and joy. I love her just as I would my very own daughter. Don't think you're going to be taking advantage of her, or sponging off of my good nature and money—"

"Sir!" Ash blurted. He paused, considering how he wanted to play his hand. Offended? Angered? Amused? He decided to go with honest. "I'm not even going to entertain your concerns. If I'm going to see your niece on a social basis, then you are going to just have to accept the situation and see for yourself that I have no ill intentions."

Bernard Oakes rolled his truculent eyes. "Typical lawyer. Nice song and dance."

The man brusquely turned and departed Ash's office, leaving the door wide open. Ash stepped forward to secure the door, again blocking the noise from the office floor. As he grasped the brass doorknob he looked out into the sea of desks with employees seated behind the majority of them. Ash was met with the wide eyes and gapping mouths of the masses. He returned to his own desk, to his open laptop, and resumed working on the brief he had been typing.

In less than a minute Ash heard a timid knock on the glass of the door. He looked up to see one of the younger administrative assistants, a cardboard box in her hands. She opened the door, thrusting the box in ahead of her.

"Here's, here's a box, Mr. Walker."

"What's that for?"

"I…I thought you might need it to pack your belongings in."

"Why would I need to do that?"

"Well…usually when someone from the top floor has a meeting with someone on this floor…they, they've been fired."

help. But he did, and as expected she bitterly stated she would manage without his or anyone else's help. He returned to the first floor to find answers to their questions from the gaggle of workmen swarming the lobby..

The electrician Ash found was talking to the technician for the elevator company, him having just finished his assessment. They estimated it would easily take forty-eight to seventy-two hours to restore the elevator service, perhaps even more depending on parts availability. Numerous components would need to be ordered, as the motor had been fried by the surge of water. The doors of the elevator shaft were parted, and two industrial fans were turned on high, circulating the air in an attempt to dry out the cinderblock elevator tower.

Ash was about to reenter the stairwell of the fire escape when he saw her—Krissy Oakes--standing in the entry of the lobby. She was wearing an inflated down parka, slender blue jeans, and a black knit hat with a large pompom on its point. *Was there nothing the woman could wear to make her look any less gorgeous?* He felt the beginning ascent of the elevator below his belt.

"What on earth happened here?" she asked, her eyes scanning all of the commotion. "I just came by to return the CDs you loaned me the other night." She held the three plastic cases up in the air.

"A ruptured water pipe." Ash projected a vivacious smile. "We're getting a new lobby!"

"Well, that's the good news." She met his kiss and returned it. "Have you had dinner yet?"

"Nah, and I can't leave here in the middle of this quagmire. We don't even have running water right now. They've said they're probably going to need to turn the power off a couple of times to repair some things."

"You can at least send out for delivery, can't you? You've got to eat."

"I've got a better idea!"

Once again going door-to-door, Ash with Krissy in tow, organized a dinner delivery of pizza and salad to all residents remaining behind. He told the tenants it was compliments of the HOA, but it was secretly paid for by Ashton Walker. Doris, a little more mellowed with her acceptance of the current situation at Parc LeMay, ordered an extra-large pizza with the intent of making several meals of it. The nearby pizzeria even threw in a complimentary dessert for each of the residents when Krissy explained the situation to the guy taking the phone order..

Ash and Krissy met the delivery driver in the half-circle driveway, him looking stoked at a potentially large tip for the $140 dollar order. The couple ran multiple trips up and down the stairwell taking orders to their respective requestor. Once all had been delivered, they took their own supreme pizza and salads into Unit 3C. A couple of bottles of beer were taken from Ash's refrigerator. They sat

"Yeah. Sure. NO!" He sat upright. He listened for the sounds of the workmen he had fallen asleep to but heard nothing more than the usual limited traffic from the street below.

"Ash, he's acting crazy! I've never seen him so, so charged up!" she resumed her whisper, grossly discordant to her whispers while they made love.

"Who? Who's acting crazy?" *Was this one of Krissy's episodes of immaturity, her seeking attention and a reaction from him like she had that evening at Trailblazers?*

"My uncle! Who else? Bernie told me about his visit to your office yesterday. And he told me he didn't want me to see you anymore. He was so angry he threw a heavy marble ashtray at me. He's never done anything physically threatening like that ever before." He could hear Krissy sniffle. "It's exactly what drove my mom away when my dad died. Bernie is, is *selective* with whom he associates with, and he expects me to be the same."

Ash immediately felt insulted by the exclusionary insinuation. Ash was now fully awake. "Krissy…I don't want to drive a wedge between you and your uncle. And he doesn't exactly sound like someone I'd choose to be around either."

"Trust me, the wedge is already there. It's been there for years. Ash, I've seen him mad before but he's, he's never been this enraged. I've locked myself in my room and I don't know if the door can stop him if he continues like this. Wait!"

Ash could hear a muffled argument amongst several voices and then what sounded like the slamming of a door. "He's...he's leaving the house... I heard the garage door open...He's, he's gone. Yeah, he's left the house."

"Get your stuff and come on over. You can stay here tonight, but *just* for tonight. I don't know that I feel comfortable with you being here long term... We've only just met."

"That didn't stop you from having sex with me last week or our little bounce in your bed a couple of hours ago." *She had him there.*

Unable to fall back asleep, Ashton Walker redressed and sat on his butt in the empty hallway, his apartment's door propped open. He heard her approaching steps echoing within the cinderblock of the stairwell and the opening of the fire escape's door in the early morning silence of the third floor. *Silence? Was Betty's television broken?* He stood and rushed to assist the woman who still looked stunning as she approached him with her mussed hair, tear streaked face and sloppy attire.

"Thanks." She handed off her carry-on bag to Ash. She maneuvered through his front door, a large, quilted duffle over her shoulder doing battle with the doorframe. *Did the woman not know how to travel light? It was only going to be for a single night, right?*

"Krissy... I'm a lawyer to my core. I cross all my *t's*, I dot all of my *i's*. Well, usually. I've been pretty sloppy with you. I...I don't know all that much about you or what I'm getting into with you—"

"Don't you have to go to work in a few hours?" She rolled away from his side of the bed. "Good night, Ashton Walker."

Her dodge sent up a red flag, causing him to get very little sleep over the next several hours.

Chapter 12

Unlikely Allegiance

Ash heard the strained voice of a rock star, screaming the lyrics to the wakeup tune he had programed on his cell phone, sounding precisely at 6:45 a.m.. This was immediately followed by a female voice releasing in a crescendo, "What in the world is that blasted noise?" Ash immediately flipped from his stomach to his back, sitting upright to see a woman lying in his bed. *Oh yeah . . .*

Krissy Oakes brought the pillow over her head. "That's your alarm tone? Seriously?" she mumbled from beneath the down feathers.

"Yeah." Ash threw his cojoined ankles from beneath the bedsheet and brought his feet to the chilled hardwood floor. Now sitting upright on the edge of the bed with his back to her he yawned, "So what's your wakeup song?"

Barely audible from beneath the pillow, she replied, "I try not to schedule anything before 10 a.m."

"Well, we *all* weren't born with a silver spoon in our pudding." He obviously wasn't a morning person either.

"Touché, mon ami." She took the corner of her pillow and soundly clobbered Ash in the back of his head.

He breathed a sigh of relief as he entered an almost vacant lobby and an empty elevator, going directly to the sixth floor without stopping. He tightly closed his eyes as the doors parted on his floor, opening one eye, half-expecting to see Uncle Bernie seated in a high back desk chair before the elevator's doors, awaiting his arrival. The relief was short-lived, Ash experiencing a gut-wrenching premonition. Perhaps the imposing man was already sitting-in-wait in Ash's own office chair. A cascade of calm and peace encompassed Ash when he looked through the closed glass door to see his chair vacant, the sanctity of his office undisturbed by the CFO.

Ash resumed his normal routine, letting his guard down only slightly. He was operating on adrenaline and the caffeine from a 20 oz. coffee purchased from a drive-through on his ride into the office. He participated in a zoom conference with the lawyer for a baby tech firm in Charlotte, North Carolina. They were actually seeking purchase from PaseoParkTechnology, instead of being the victim of the usual hunt and kill by the technology giant. Ash took great pleasure in informing them of the fact they weren't qualified to be *a keeper* quite yet, him tossing them back to fight another day in the ocean of tech firms.

He stayed in the confines of his glass office for the entire five hours of his day. He didn't even venture out for his usual 2:30 coffee break with Matt. Matt was still out of town leaving him with no one to chat with in the large open cafeteria...more like no one there to protect him or to serve as a witness.

Ashton Walker envisioned Matt in the capacity of his ever-vigilant bodyguard, watching for a sneak attack by Bernard Oakes. Ash could almost hear Matt's, "Oakes at 2 o'clock! Take cover!" And the two of them in their business suits dropping and rolling under the cafeteria table, taking shelter from Bernard Oakes's venomous tongue or perhaps a marble ashtray being lobbed at them by the CFO.

With the clicking of the SEND icon, Ash ended his day. He retrieved his topcoat from the back of his door and headed out into the late autumn chill, warmed by the knowledge Krissy Oakes would be there waiting for him in his 1,212 square foot apartment. He thought he could get used to it, her being there every evening, a gin and tonic in hand as he came through the front door. Yeah, he would welcome her company. But just not this evening. As soon as he entered his condo he was going to send her home to make amends with Uncle Bernie. He couldn't live on the edge another day as he had done today, always looking over his shoulder. It was way too stressful.

The elevator shaft was still drying out from the ruptured water pipe, forcing Ash to take the fire stairs from the basement garage to his third floor. Puffing slightly from the three-story climb, he pulled the heavy metal fire door open into the stairwell and turned to his right, towards his unit. The sight he was met with cause him to lose his grip on his satchel, the leather bag almost reaching the dirty carpet of the hallway.

"Hello Ashton Walker." That magnificent smile, maybe even a little larger than usual, couldn't totally mask her embarrassment at being caught in the wrong.

Krissy was wearing an oversized pair of athletic shorts, taken from a drawer in Ash's dresser, and her own sloppy sweater. She was seated cross-legged on the floor just outside of Ash's opened front door. Across the hallway was Doris Pitman, sitting on one of her dining room chairs, obstructing the door to her own unit.

"Ashton," came Doris's consistent gravely greeting.

"Ladies." His mistrusting eyes traveled between the two women.

"We've been having the best conversation," bubbled Krissy.

"Did you know your friend has played the piano on the stage of Carnegie Hall?" asked Doris, like she actually knew the reputation of Carnegie Hall and of those invited to perform there.

"I don't believe I've heard this story." Ash's eyes narrowed giving Krissy a look, him chastising her inability to follow a simple directive to stay within the confines of his condo. He found he didn't like having his orders defied, especially when it was for her own safety.

"I won a competition, and the prize was to play on one of the stages at Carnegie. It was really no big deal. It wasn't like I had top billing."

"Impressive," Ashton manifested an exaggerated facial expression of amazement and wonder.

"And did you know Doris was a member of 4-H when she was a girl, and she still has the ribbons for her prize cows in her condo?" Krissy quickly added, "But I haven't seen them! I told her I'm grounded and I can't leave your condo."

"I believe this hallway isn't part of my property." His blood pressure had started to return to normal, but it again spiked with his returning thoughts of Bernie Oakes and his duly noted lunacy. "I asked you to stay inside with the door locked for your own safety. Was that asking too much of you?" He felt like a father chastising his middle school daughter.

"I can be inside and have the door locked in 2.25 seconds." As if she were an enlistee in a Marine boot camp, she performed a sideways roll of her slender body, stopping just on the other side of the door frame. She rose to her knees and slammed the door shut. The setting of the door's lock was audible in the hallway. The door reopened and Krissy crawled back into the hall on her hands and knees. When once again seated on her butt she matter-of-factly stated, "Doris timed me."

"You are hopeless." Ash couldn't help but laugh.

God, he loved Krissy's gray-blue eyes. Maybe she really wasn't ditzy. Maybe she was just unorthodox, refreshing...fun. *Had he ever been fun? Had fun? Allowed fun into his own life?*

Ash and Krissy excused themselves with Doris dragging her dining room chair back into her condo. As Ash entered the open space of the living/dining room combination, he smelled the delightful odors of sautéed garlic and herbs.

"Wow! What smells so good?"

"I see you are a culinary minimalist, but I did find the ingredients to make baked ziti and a pathetic salad...wilted lettuce and Ranch dressing." Krissy could be heard opening and closing the few drawers in search of utensils. She began setting cutlery next to the two dinner plates.

"I'm just thrilled I don't have to cook tonight. It's my least favorite thing to do in life."

"Well, I for one, love to cook. It's my therapy. But then I have to run a couple of miles to work the calories off." She stood back to assess her handiwork. "Glasses? What do you like to drink with your dinner?"

"There's a bottle of cheap wine in the back of my fridge."

"Perfect!"

Ash changed out of his business attire into his off-the-clock ensemble of blue jeans and a rugby shirt, seeing the shirt more apropos than one of his usual sweatshirts. He went into the master bath and added a slight spritz of his aftershave to his throat hoping the woman, whom he could now hear setting the hot casserole on his dining room table, would find the scent enticing.

In all honesty, he didn't know if he had the strength or the energy for sex again tonight, his stamina drained by the stress and sleeplessness of the past couple of days.

Chapter 13

An Extended Staycation

As they ate the Italian dinner with its limited ingredients Krissy sprang from the table, bounding to the credenza just inside the front door. She took a battered white envelope from the distressed stack of maple drawers that once housed maps or blueprints, but currently served as a credenza.

"A lady dropped this off for you today. Her name was…Colleen?"

"Corinne?"

"Yeah, Corinne."

"So you opened the door for her too, today?" he chastised.

"No. She slipped it under the door," followed by an insulant protrusion of her tongue. "I told her I was quarantined and couldn't open the door."

The envelope was opened, the piece of stationery removed. He unfolded it to see a handwritten note in an almost inscrutable font. He read the travesty, a blend of grammatical and spelling errors, to the best of his ability.

"What is it?" Krissy asked.

"It's from my housekeeper. She was…is one of six kids, and they were split up into foster homes when she was really young. I told her I would try to help her find her siblings." He held the paper up to the light of the chandelier, finding it of no help with the translating.

"That can be a horrendous undertaking. Are you sure you have the time to do it?" Krissy took a second helping of the casserole, a string of melted cheese refusing to let go of the serving spoon. "And the woman didn't look like she has the means to pay you for your time. Her shoes were about to fall apart, they were so worn out."

"I told her I'd do it pro bono." Ash took on a look of consternation. "How would you know what Corinne's shoes looked like?"

"Okay. So I opened the door, just a crack." She threw her hands up in surrender, spying melted cheese on the back of one hand while doing so. Krissy licked the wayward cheese from her hand. "Now aren't you the saintly one, doing pro bono work."

Again pursuing the letter, "Well, from the list of siblings' names who she could still remember and their locations, I've got my work cut out for me… I think she's going to be gravely disappointed… She has two brothers and a sister listed: Horace Collins, last seen in Cuba, Missouri. Grady Collins, last seen in St. James, Missouri. And… I can't quite make this out…Clarise? Cloris? No last name, in Camdenton, Missouri. The best she can figure is Horace is 60 to 65, Grady is 73 to 78 and *Chlorine* or whatever the heck her name is…" Ash stopped to bring the paper closer to his face as he squinted at the numbers. "…is 70 to 80 years old?"

"It could be a fun project, kind of a challenge."

"I guess I need to find the county courthouses for these bergs and see what kind of records they maintain; births, deaths, et cetera."

"Like I said, you've got a job ahead of you. Maybe I can help. I do have two semesters of Wohlwend Hall Law School under my belt." She finished with a loud eye roll.

"Right now… I'll do the dishes and you can pack your belongings, go home, and make nice with Uncle Bernie."

"Uncle Bernie isn't even home, and he won't be for the next four or five days. He's attending the wedding of my step aunt's sister in the Hamptons this coming weekend." Seeing the annoyed look overtaking Ash's face, she playfully cowered, bringing her hands to cover her drawn-in lips. "Didn't I tell you that last night?"

"No, I think you failed to mention that little fact. Here I spent the entire day on heightened alert for nothing, expecting to be ambushed by Bernie and he wasn't even in the building!" The rivet of anger that had pierced his body quickly subsided into bliss filled relief with the realization that there was no need for Kristin Oakes to return to an empty house. The pajama party in Unit 3C could continue for almost an entire week with Uncle Bernie away in the Hamptons… *Maybe she had planned this all along, an extended stay being the reason for her abundance of luggage brought with her in the night.*

Meredith caught her breath, "Is this the girl I stashed the bottle of wine in your refrig for when you come home from Seattle?"

"See you Thanksgiving Day if not before, Mere. Bye, bye." Ash knew the exact expression on his little sister's face with his abrupt end to their phone call, her question left unanswered.

The lovers entered the bedroom. As they sensually disrobed, the Thanksgiving dinner plan was confirmed. Ashton couldn't wait to show off his prize to his sister.

***

For the next five days Krissy and Ashton negotiated through the transition of their relationship from temporary co-workers to what could only be referred to as roommates with benefits. He spent his days in his office at PaseoParkTechnology and she spent her days breaking the rules of the condominium's Home Owner's Association.

During mail retrieval in the condominium's lobby and conversations on the stairwell landings while delivering packages to the residents, Ash had heard from his neighbors, complaints of his sound system being played too loud, about ladies' undergarments being hung to dry on his balconies, amongst other smaller infractions of the rules for the residents. He was met with bewildered looks from those who knew Ash as a quiet, respectful person who exercised social decorum.

"Who is the leggy ash blonde in skimpy little shorts, utilizing the fire stairwell to do laps?" Ash promised his neighbors he would make his visitor aware of her unacceptable actions, as he simultaneously tried to instill that she really was a good person at heart.

"Krissy, we have…rules to live by here," he cautiously began on the third night of her staycation. "I'm on the homeowner's board so I have to abide by and I have to enforce these rules."

Ash entered the condo's tiny kitchen to see two large stockpots, neither belonging to him, being stirred by the alluring woman dressed in black leggings and a slenderizing top, a deep V exposing her cleavage. He restrained his hands from going in for a voluptuous breast, each. Instead he breathed in the most amazing smells of herbs and broth, permeating the surrounding air.

"Do the rules serve a purpose?" she asked.

"All rules serve some purpose."

"I think your rules, or your HOA rules, are ludicrous."

"Let me get this… So you're saying I can blare my sound system at 2 a.m.?"

"Of course not! People are sleeping . . . or trying to sleep."

"Krissy…everyone is old in this building…They aren't living on a clock anymore. They sleep when they want to, get up when they want to…and they respect each other enough to give their neighbors the same courtesy." Ash couldn't believe he was having this discussion with a twenty-three-year-old woman, but realized it wasn't her age but probably her privileged upbringing that made her oblivious to the lives and needs of other people.

"Okay, okay. I see your point." She scraped the scraps from the cutting board into the trashcan and turned to stir one of the bubbling pots.

"What are you making? Where did you get those huge pots?" He leaned over Krissy's shoulder to peek into one of the bubbling cauldrons.

"This one belongs to Vi and this one belongs to… to Jerry. I'm making Stone Soup."

"What? How did you get pots from Vi and Jerry? How did you even know they had them? And you and I can't eat this much soup in our lifetime! What kind of soup? Did you say, *stone* soup?"

"I take it you've never heard the story, 'Stone Soup'?" she asked, upon seeing Ash's perplexed expression. "You've obviously had a deprived childhood. Every kindergartener has heard this story! It's about a starving soldier going into a small war-ravaged village, looking for something to eat. No one wants to feed him, so he cons the villagers into at least giving him some items for him to make a pot of stone soup. The villagers all want to see how he makes soup from a stone. So one person gives him carrots, another potatoes, another one—"

Chapter 14

Now We Give Thanks

Monday morning: the first day of the short work week with Thanksgiving at its culmination. Ash returned to his normal routine, arriving at his desk at PaseoParkTechnology at his usual 8:20 a.m. During this morning's drive he mentally readied himself for the inevitable: a visit from Bernard Oakes. He didn't know when, he didn't know where. He just knew it wasn't going to be pretty.

Krissy Oakes had returned to her own room in the home of Bernard Oakes the prior afternoon. She entered the stately house through the back door, directly into the kitchen with its showroom ambiance, immaculately clean as a result of little use by the residents of the house. Krissy listened for the commotion of her uncle and step-aunt coming from the second floor, them unpacking from their trip East, but heard only the ticking of the clock above the kitchen sink and the dump of the ice maker. She took her quilted duffle through the furnishings of the staged first floor, the décor intended to impress and not embrace visitors to the house. She bounded upward to her bedroom on the second level. Upon entering her bedroom with its French Provincial furniture painted in its camo pattern, she dropped her duffle to the floor.

Her breath caught in her throat. The drawers of the pistachio and mauve dresser had been ransacked and the clothing of her closet was strewn across the bedroom's floor. Panic gripped her body. She listened again, this time for the sounds of an intruder. Were they still in the house, destroying other rooms in search of whatever they desired? She fled back into the second-floor hallway, spinning to peer into the open doors of the remaining bedrooms in an attempt to assess the damage to the additional rooms, but she saw no vandalism through the open doors. The only room exhibiting a chaotic upheaval was her room.

Returning to her room, she snatched her duffle from the hardwood floor. It was then she saw the note laying on her pillow. She ripped the madly scribbled edict from the bedspread, her eyes racing across its few lines. Uncle Bernie's handwriting stated "if she continued to see Ashton *Warner*" Krissy would never reside in Bernard Oakes's house again… "No problem," she gave an insolent laugh. She'd just live with Ashton *Walker*, instead.

Ash didn't know how or when his confrontation with Bernard Oakes would transpire. He just knew it would occur if he continued to work at PaseoParkTechnology and Krissy continued to reside in 3C. He joined the other employees shuffling across the terrazzo floor of the lobby. He barely heard the greeting of a law clerk as he waited for the elevator to return to the first floor, its doors open and sucking in the dozen or so employees. His mind raced with speculative scenarios as to how his day was going to play out.

Ash thought about emailing *Rules of War*, much like the Geneva Conference with its humanitarian stipulations to Mr. Oakes. What would he demand?

*No sudden attacks.

*Nothing in public view...or at the urinals in the men's room.

*Voices kept in a normal speaking range.

*No cheap shots. Only constructive talking points allowed.

*The taking of Kristin Oakes as a hostage was strictly forbidden. She would be able to ambulate at her own freewill...She probably would do that anyway.

The morning passed tediously slow, but without incident. Ash ventured down to the first-floor cafeteria for his morning coffee. Surrounded by the stainless steel and glass of the cafeteria, he took quick glances around the eatery, no Bernard Oakes in sight. A few other associates milled before the coffee service, barely acknowledging Ash's presence. He chose one of the throwaway cups, taking a matching lid. He did this in lieu of his usual white ceramic cup, imbibed leisurely at one of the tables overlooking the manicured lawn of the building. The absence of Matt, out on vacation for the week, left Ash feeling venerable, an easy target for the CFO.

Approaching the elevator in the lobby with the intent to return to the sixth floor, his throwaway coffee cup in hand, Ash saw Bernard Oakes in the company of the firm's CEO and the President of the Board of Trustee's. Ash felt the building of his inner bravado and a sense of protection with Uncle Bernie being in the company of his peers. The three men stood before the closed elevator doors, a lighthearted conversation in play as evidenced by the throaty laughs of the men. Surly Bernie wouldn't do anything foolish, jeopardizing his own career and reputation when in the presence of his compadres...*would he?* Ash moved swiftly to join the threesome in the confines of the small room soon to be gliding upward. *Bring it on, Uncle Bernie.*

"Gentlemen," Ash acknowledged the three dignitaries with a nod of his head as they turned to face the elevator's doors in a synchronized movement indicative of much practice. The threesome's bonding was obvious as they smugly looked at the young man invading their elevator. "Six please," he smoothly requested.

"Six it is." And the CEO pushed the illuminated six. He shopped Ash, taking a quick assessment of his physical appearance, his professional air. "Sixth Floor, the Legal Department. Keeping the firm on the straight and narrow. Keep up the good work."

"Yes sir." Ash couldn't resist. "Morning, Mr. Oakes."

"Walker."

Ash raised his eyes to scan the digital numbers passing above his head. The man had remembered his last name correctly but probably had now forgotten his *odd* first name. But Ash could tell he was most definitely on the CFO's radar. His curt delivery of his greeting told Ash the battle had only just begun. *Yeah, bring it on, Oakes!* But nothing more occurred that day.

Krissy again refused to ever return to the home of Bernard Oakes that evening as she and Ash shared the delivered meal from the nearby barbecue joint. Krissy retold, verbatim, the phone call she had received following the exchange in the building's elevator. Uncle Bernie had a scathing phone conversation with the young lady reconfirming his lack of esteem for the commoner whom she currently chose to side with. Bernie had demanded she return to his home immediately. Would that make her a hostage? Had The Rules of War been breached, and a stalemate was now in place?

Ash took a stir-crazy Krissy to the trendy supermarket on the corner of 13th and Main in downtown Kansas City that evening. It was a more upscale grocery store than the Price King his elderly neighbors preferred and where he usually did his own shopping. He and Krissy roamed the aisles, her selecting items that Ash had no idea of their taste or purpose. Spices that had strange names and expensive prices along with produce from exotic places and foreign to his midwestern culinary skills now filled their shopping cart. Krissy had a plethora of recipes in her head, and she filled their cart with the ingredients necessary to make Ashton Walker a happy and well-fed man. They picked up a few bottles of wine to complete the nightly meals along with the ingredients to actually make the dinner rolls requested by Meredith for Thanksgiving.

As they rode back to the condo, Krissy opened the conversation. "Your family. You said your parents are deceased?"

Ash sighed. He slowed for the yellow light, the red appearing within seconds. "Yeah. I was fifteen, Meredith was thirteen, the ages when we needed our parents the most. You remember hearing about a plane crash outside of Brussels two weeks before Christmas, seventeen...eighteen years ago? Maybe not...you would have been just a little kid. My parents were on that plane, on an anniversary trip. 'Happy Anniversary to you'." he bitterly sang the line to the tune of Happy Birthday. He looked at the car to his left not wanting Krissy's sympathy, but her empathy. This was one thing they had in common, a bond of sorts; the pain of dead parents, gone too soon in their relatively young lives..

"I'm so sorry. Why couldn't our parents pass peacefully in their sleep? A boating accident and a plane crash. Seems like everyone else's parents go without so much fanfare." She reached across the center console of his car and briefly rested her hand on his thigh in solidarity.

"My Grandma Emma, my mom's mom, moved in with Meredith and me. She did an amazingly fine job of parental substitution, although I'm sure she would have preferred her mahjong group and bridge club to raising two teenagers. And the insurance settlement from the airline and my parents' policies put my sister and me through college and made a substantial down payment on my condo. Then Meredith got married, and her husband was killed in a motorcycle accident almost five years ago. My family definitely doesn't possess a good mojo." Ash sped up to make the next traffic light before it too became red.

"Jesus…" Krissy gave a shudder at the consistency of bad luck in the Walker family.

***

So Monday and Tuesday at PaseoParkTechnology were relatively uneventful. Wednesday was also uneventful…until 3 p.m. that afternoon. Ash heard the woosh of his office door, the visitor again finding no need to even knock and wait for permission to enter.

"Walker." The same challenging tone of voice in play. Today, Bernard Oakes didn't feel the need to be formal, appearing in his shirt sleeves. But he still struck a touch of terror into the heart and soul of Ashton Walker with his clenched fists dangling at his side.

"Mr. Oakes…What can I do for you?" Ash debated rising from his desk, but found comfort and protection being seated behind the solid wood construction.

The man studied his shoes for a few brief seconds then fixed his glare on Ashton Walker. "My wife is expecting Kristen at our house for Thanksgiving dinner tomorrow at noon."

"Well, that will be a bit of a challenge, sir, since Krissy will be having Thanksgiving dinner with me and my family at that exact same time." He tossed the pencil he had been holding onto the desk top as if throwing down his gloves and taking up the challenge in a duel. He wondered where in his Rules of War did the negotiations for family seniority and the mandatory attendance of events fall?

The man was silent. A distinct redness began traveling up his neck from the collar of his white dress shirt, merging into his earlobes and causing tiny beads of sweat to develop at his temples. He shifted his weight and cleared his throat in a reset of his temper, barely under control. He brought his palms together as if smashing a wad of paper.

"I'm sure my wife can move our feast to the dinner hour since it will just be the four of us. Will six o'clock work for Krissy…and you?"

Ash's brain went immediately on the defensive. Was there going to be an ambush, an attack as he walked into the CFO's house tomorrow evening with Krissy Oakes on his arm? He'd need to strategically plan this event with Krissy, discussing the option of possible fallout and an agreed upon response. He'd need to stall for time until he could do a thorough reconnaissance of the situation, a

"Hopefully, Ash will bring you back again and often," replied Meredith, her kids flanking her sides and taking playful swats at each other behind her back. Meredith gave Ash the nod of approval that only siblings could successfully intercept and interpret.

"Maybe Ash and I can host Christmas, and you can come to his place."

An immediate iciness descended over the farewell banter of the threesome. Meredith formed a fragile smile. "We'll...we'll see. Yes...that would be nice."

Oh, yeah, Krissy cringed. *Plane crash. Dead parents. Two weeks before Christmas. Ouch.*

Ash, driving the sporty car belonging to Kristen Oakes, headed for the residence of Bernard and Hillary Oakes. Having driven only a matter of blocks, Krissy broke the strained silence in the roadster. "I'm so sorry about my impromptu Christmas invitation to Meredith. I absolutely didn't make the connection between the holidays and your parents. I feel so bad.

"It's not important. Mere and I are used to it. Life goes on." His words didn't mesh with the pained expression on his face, visible to Krissy in his profile.

"So, do you put up a tree or anything? Go to parties? Anything?" Her hand was tenderly placed on his thigh once again.

"I don't, and it's probably more so because no one else will see the tree but me. And I'm not much on parties anyway. But Meredith decorates because of the kids. Over the past few years it has become a real challenge for her with her husband gone too. But the kids deserve a tree and to celebrate like their friends do. She tries to make it normal for them even though they are struggling too." Ash pause, taking a sideways glance at Krissy. "I bet you just love Christmas."

"Yeah, I do. Not so much for the religious aspect, but for the levity and change of attitude in people. Even Uncle Bernie goes from being Ebenezer Scrooge to being a nice guy." She gave an insecure laugh, "It's really kind of scary."

"Maybe I'll have to give it some thought and reconsider my position." He looked up to see the gates parted at the entry to the street of stately residences that the Oakes house sat amongst.

Ashton Walker took a deep breath as he turned off the car's motor in the driveway before the behemoth home of Bernard Oakes. He felt eyes watching him from the large picture window as he passed the front of the car to open the passenger door of Kristen Oakes. He tried to walk with confidence, appearing in charge of his destiny, but in truth feeling out of control, him being on unfamiliar turf. He once again entertained thoughts that Kristin Oakes was out of his league, him unworthy of a woman such as her. He fought the feelings. *I am worthy, I am worthy.*

"Well, here we are," she said with a weak smile as she stepped from the car. "Got your mace and brass knuckles ready?"

"My blood type is O+ and I'm an organ donor," he teased back.

The heavy oak front door swung into the house and a perky young lady with short, chopped hair in silver gray with a purple overtone was dancing in the doorway. "Heeey, Krissy!"

"Heeey, Hilly!"

The sorority sisters were locked in a rolling hug, reverting to their days at Brighton College.

Krissy clutched Ash's bicep between her hands, "Hilly, this is Ashton Walker."

"Just Ash." He extended his hand but was immediately encompassed in a warm hug.

"You better be good to Krissy. I've got connections in New York, and they'll break your knee caps if you aren't." Hilly did a very good imitation of a New York mobster, accent and all.

"I'm a lawyer. I'll sue." Ash playfully sneered his response.

"Yeah, right, now there's a threat!" she discounted. "They're all lawyers too!"

Ash looked up to see Bernard Oakes standing in the open door. Dressed casually in a plaid shirt and khakis, he released a warm, "Well there's my girl" along with a hug of Krissy as he met her on the sidewalk. Ash, no longer feeling improperly dressed, took a cleansing breath, encouraging his anxiety to slightly dissipate. Bernie extended his right hand along with a "Good to see you again, Ash. Glad you could make it." And it was Ash, just Ash. Not "Walker," usually spoken more as a threat and not as a welcoming acknowledgement. The man was turning into a real Jekyll and Hyde.

The foursome, sat in the formal dining room, the table displaying Rosenthal china and Waterford stemware, and enjoyed a bountiful dinner. It was obviously professionally catered with its over-the-top level of presentation. The turkey wore those little white paper hats on its stumps. The dressing had oysters within. And the cranberries were baked with almond slivers and coconut…The tube of jellied cranberries served at Ash's sister's house still exhibited the lines from the tin can they came in. Ash didn't know if he'd ever be able to eat another frozen turkey and dressing dinner, him now being tainted by this experience. Every bite of the Oakes' Thanksgiving dinner screamed *opulence*.

"Let me give you a tour of the house," Uncle Bernie offered to *Ash* as he took his last bite of pumpkin pie. *Was that Pappy Van Winkle he tasted in the pie filling?*

"I'd like that." Ash was overcome with an immediate feeling of dread. "Will Krissy be joining us?" *Is this how I will die, locked in the basement? Buried in the garden?*

Bernard Oakes's firm "No" made Ash think his concerns just might be a distinct possibility. He wished he had formally filed his Last Will and Testament with the county clerk, now moving the item up on his to-do list if he survived this evening.

The two men walked room to room in the large Tudor style home in the fashionable area of older Kansas City. Bernard Oakes pointed out paintings purchased in Paris, tapestries from Portugal, and art glass from Venice. He'd occasionally stop and study a work with a new appreciation, and then would resume his calculated pace down another hallway, into another wing of the mammoth house. Reaching his study, Bernie pointed to an uncomfortable chair and commanded, "Sit." He went to the bar in a dim corner of the study and poured two glasses of brandy, passing one to Ash.

"I'm sure Krissy has told you plenty of… of things about me. In my own defense, I won't deny I can be a real tyrant at times. But your *girlfriend* can be a real handful too." Bernard Oakes protruded his lower lip and looked over the lower rims of his brown eyes, him seeking confirmation that his own image was being reassessed in the mind of Ashton Walker. "I've had to pick her up from hospital emergency rooms, juvenile detention facilities, and more times than I can count from wild parties and raves." A tip of his head signified his closing remark to be true and factual.

"Krissy?" Ash scoffed.

"Kristin Louise Oakes, to be exact."

"No…" Suddenly, Ash had a flashback to his first conversation with Kristin Louise Oakes on the parking lot of PaseoParkTechnology, the conversation in which she spouted off the list of genitalia-driven mascot names from Paske Community College. He was now convinced by this new evidence she had done this for shock value, trying to get a response from him. Face it: even negative attention is still attention. "Yes sir. You may be on to something."

"But tonight while we were stuffing our faces, I saw a different young woman. This one is happy, secure and balanced… Keep her that way, Ash. Don't let her revert to the flake she was becoming. She's too bright and, and capable to be a bimbo. God knows, Hillary has the bimbo thing down to an artform."

Ash felt the sip he had just taken of the expensive brandy begin to burn with its descent. He gave a quick cough to temper the sensation. "I'll try, sir. I'm finding myself becoming very fond of her."

The gentlemen left the study with a fresh brandy in hand, Bernie challenging Ash to a game of billiards in the game room with its dark paneling and menagerie of taxidermized heads hanging from the walls. As the evening progressed, Ash also found himself becoming more comfortable in the company of the CFO. Their conversation melted into a relaxed discussion of civil issues and current politics, the one-time inhibiting man sharing opinions that surprisingly closely matched those of Ash.

"Have you considered where you'd like to be in the next five, ten years with PPT?" Bernie removed the triangle from the balls.

"PPT?" Ash always referred to it as PaseoParkTechnology, the full title required by the legal department in all of their dealings. "Oh! PPT… No, no. I've just always thought of myself as a lawyer, but perhaps I could see myself as Head of Legal in about twenty years."

"A young man like you should have more ambition." Bernie chided as he watched Ash break, a striped ball heading for a corner pocket.

"I…I… I guess I'm just comfortable where I am." Ash took the square of chalk and gave his cue a coating. He wondered if Bernard Oakes could detect his inner feelings of inadequacy, his lack of motivation… his need for consistency and comfort while secretly searching for excitement and adventure.

"Well, start thinking about it." Bernie watched as the white ball was planted in a side pocket by the novice with a pool cue.

As a now sanctioned couple, they left the home of Bernie and Hilly Oakes and headed back to downtown Kansas City, to the condominium of Ash Walker and Krissy Oakes. The trunk of the roadster and Krissy's lap were filled with more of the clothing and belongings of Krissy to be moved into the condo. It would probably take both Ash and Krissy multiple trips between the lower-level garage and his third-floor unit with the building's elevator still out of service.

But Ash Walker didn't care. He wasn't alone any more. He had someone of his very own. And he had something to think about: a promotion to the top floor of PPT in his not-so-distant future.

Chapter 15

Tis the Season

With Ash's blessing, Krissy Oakes visited the live tree lot on the grounds of St. Michael's Church. The smell of the cut pine trees hung in the chilly morning air. She selected a timber from the temporary racks belonging to the church's Boy Scout troop, bringing it to its full height then twisting it to expose a deal-killing bald spot. The defective balsam was returned to the rack. Finally the perfect tree was selected and the jubilant, yet semi-frozen Boy Scout did his duty by carrying the tree to the sales trailer and assisting in the netting of the branches by the Pack Leader. She brought home the seven-foot balsam tree, tied to the roof of her roadster, almost dragging its top bough on the pavement.

She purchased ornaments and garland from the nearest big box store. She vacillated between all-white and multicolored twinkle lights, opting for the latter, thinking them more cheerful on the tree. A few boxes of mylar tinsel was tossed into the shopping cart for good measure. She bought artificial pine roping and large red bows for the railings of both balconies of the condo unit. An appropriately sized wreath was the final purchase to be hung on the front door of Unit 3C.

Pushing the red shopping cart down the aisle of gift wraps, she'd pull an occasional tube from its box, eyeing the designs and patterns on the rolls of holiday gift wrap. She was looking for the perfect paper that would reignite the joy of

Christmas in the heart of Ashton Walker. She looked at some patterns as too childish and others as just plain bizarre. She settled on a geometric design of triangular trees and bold stars, the colors true to the holiday. A couple of bags of bows was tossed into the cart.

Wondering aimlessly down a nearby aisle Krissy added eleven gift boxes with samplings of cheeses and sausage from a holiday display, one for each resident of the condo building. She pushed the cart towards the cashier's lanes, tubes of gift wrap projecting upward from the four corners, resembling the stacks on a tractor trailer truck. An elderly gentleman shopping with his wife made a quip about the pretty young lady being Santa's helper, as he chivalrously stooped to pick up a bag of bows that had fallen from her overloaded cart.

Krissy nabbed a ladies spa basket from a display at the end of the checkout aisle for Corinne Collins, the housekeeper still in Ash's employ. A promise from Ash to embark on Corinne's sibling search with the start of the new year would be an additional part of her gift. Ash had yet to begin his research, fearing he had gotten himself into a deep hole, the task being beyond his capability.

Ash arrived home from work to find the lights of the living room dimmed. The decorated tree was tucked in the corner by the French doors to the balcony, fully illuminated with the colorful flickering lights. A scented candle was doing its best to enhance the smell of the pine tree, and Krissy had a radio station already programmed with a steady flow of Christmas carols playing softly in the background.

"Wow... I'd forgotten how pretty Christmas trees can be." He mustered a smile, making it almost to the *sincere* level.

"You like it?"

"Yeah, yeah. I like it." He dropped his satchel and joined her, standing by the tree. He took her into his arms. "And I like you."

"I like me too," came her silly retort. She returned his kiss, and another one and another one. "I thought we'd go out tonight and grab a quick dinner, and then we can shop for Christmas gifts for Meredith and the kids. If we have time I can look for something for Bernie and Hilly."

"Can I ask you something?"

"Sure."

"I know you said you have a trust fund, but you spend an awful lot of money, and you don't have a job..."

"Don't worry your head with numbers. I'm good. Uncle Bernie invested well for me and I'm enjoying the results."

"As long as you're good with it, I'm good with it."

And as long as it wasn't his checkbook or credit card, it made it all the better.

***

Ash went into his office early the Monday morning following the holiday weekend. Stepping from the elevator on the sixth floor, he saw Matt Blaylock having returned from an emergency business trip that took him out of town the Friday after Thanksgiving. Leaning against his office door frame awaiting Ash's arrival, Matt began a purposeful walk in Ash's direction, picking up speed like a locomotive.

"So, did I miss anything while I was in beautiful downtown Cleveland?" He rubbed his hands cunningly together as he flopped into his waiting chair. He was met with the wayward spring of the cushion, now trying to avoid its rude poke with a shimmy of his hips.

"Like what?" Ash tossed his scarf and gloves on to his desk and began unbuttoning his overcoat.

"Like the fact you had Thanksgiving dinner at the CFO's home." Matt tipped back to place his ankles on the edge of the desk.

"How did you hear about that?"

"All of the admins around here are buzzing about it." Matt's arms smugly folded across his chest. "Seems Bernie's secretary told another secretary, who told another secretary she overheard a heated conversation between Bernie and his wife. Something about Thanksgiving dinner and, and being welcoming to this guy, *Ashton*... How many Ashtons work in this building? Had to be you. Right?"

"Yeah, so I ate turkey and dressing with the CFO." Ash took the remote for the window shades from his desk drawer and brought them lower to allow the early morning light from the gray sky into his office.

"And you're shagging his niece. Way to go, Junior!"

Ash, about to sit in his desk chair, stood militarily straight. "I...I don't appreciate your terminology. I, I really like, and I respect Kristin. I expect you to do the same." Ash stared down his associate.

Matt stood and raised his open palms in surrender. "Okay. I'm down with that." He turned the direction of his own office, doing a little strut as he passed through the doorframe. Ash heard Matt's parting words, "Man, you've got it bad."

***

Corinne Collins's cleaning day in the condo of Ash Walker changed from Saturdays to Tuesdays. Meredith had a commercial client needing the weekend slot since their business was closed those two days. The office job was an easy task for Corinne with the office space being empty and without distractions, along with paying very well. And Corinne definitely needed the money. Meredith had received legal documents demanding she garner a part of Corinne's wages to cover an outstanding debt.

Tuesday morning, precisely at 9 a.m., Krissy opened the door to the downhearted woman, the usual plastic bucket of cleaning supplies in hand. Corinne's eyes widened, not expecting to be met by a stunning young lady who already looked well put together at the early morning hour.

"Hi! I'm Krissy, Ash's girlfriend…We met the other day when you delivered the letter to Ash. I, I live here now," she said, testing for the woman's reaction to having to clean up after a second person.

Corinne merely nodded and using an upward body thrust, motioned for Krissy to scoot out of her way. "I like to start in the kitchen."

"Fine. Let me know if you need anything."

Krissy, feeling somewhat rejected, perhaps a little judged, returned to Ash's spare bedroom used as an office. She opened her own laptop and requested the website for the city of Camdenton, Missouri. She surfed the skeletal information provided about the small town with its population of 3,718 people. Pop-ups for connecting sites plagued her computer screen. She scanned the many ads for the Lake of the Ozarks and the surrounding tourist activities.

One website, its purpose the shopping of travel arrangements particularly the listings for overnight accommodations in or near Camdenton, sparked a shiver of excitement. Serving as her guide, Krissy looked at the number of stars rating the local hotels and motels. She selected the seediest accommodations yet obviously still meeting the local Health Department's minimum standards to remain in business. *Only two stars and some seething reviews. Perfect.* She booked a room for two for three nights. *This could be fun*, she concluded.

Krissy listened as the crushed woman continued to clean the condo, moving pieces of furniture, dust mopping the hardwood floor, and then returning the pieces to their designated place. Krissy thought it somewhat rude and presumptuous that the woman had turned on the sound system of Ashton Walker. Had Ash given her his permission? She heard a single voice, singing a lilting piece, the words being those of a bleak Christmas carol. Krissy attempted to be undetected as she moved into the doorway of the home office and peeked towards the living room.

"You have an amazing voice!" Krissy skated in her sock feet towards the living room, catching herself before she totally lost her balance.

"Tha. . . thank you. God gave it to me and not much else." Corrine didn't look up from the pattern she was mopping in, following the planks of the hardwood floor. She gave a disapproving glance in the direction of the Christmas tree, taking an estimate of the number of pine needles already littering the floor.

"Have you ever sung anywhere professionally?"

"No, no. I've never had a hankerin' to stand up before a lot of people."

"You could be in a chorus, like with the symphony." Krissy moved swiftly out of the dust mop's path as it made a direct attack on her toes.

As they lay side-by-side in the afterglow, Krissy relayed the events of her relatively eventless day. She recapped the cleaning job of Corrine Collins and the conversation between them. And she talked about the online transaction which took place in the home office. That was indeed newsworthy. Ash finished the gin and tonic resting on the ebony ledge of the bed as he listened.

"I figure it could be a good starting place. Maybe even save some work or grief." She did a downward trace of his bare sternum with her fingernail.

"Can't hurt I guess. I wonder how accurate those test kits are?" He grabbed her hand before it could continue much further beyond his navel. She retracted her hand, then made a playful attack, him contracting into a protective ball in response. "Stop it!" He grasped both of her hands and brought them to his lips for a kiss.

"Well, I just went with the first DNA company that came up online. I didn't have time to do any research, so we'll see. It was on sale for $49, so it's not like I'm out a lot of money."

"Yeah, I really don't know where to start searching except for Camdenton, and I don't think they'll have very much to work with. This all happened before computers and databanks."

Krissy brought her bare breasts against Ash's chest. "Well, I booked us three nights in the Prince Edward Motel outside of Camdenton, near the Lake. I believe

PaseoParkTechnology gives their people two personal days. I hope you haven't used yours yet."

"Am I really that anal retentive? You can tell just from being with me a short amount of time that I have perfect attendance?" He raised up, as she rolled on to her back. From his elbows, he twisted to look at her in awe of her beauty.

Her pointed index finger traced his mouth. "I love my men...anal."

There was the kinky, off-the-wall side of Kristin Oakes that made her so doggone desirable to the straight arrow lying in bed beside her.

***

It was Christmas morning, the light of dawn yet to be visible between the parted drapes of the master bedroom's balcony. Krissy was sitting on the side of the bed she now claimed as her own, her knees brought up beneath her chin and watching the sleeping lawyer. She felt the bed rock as he listed to his side. A single eye of the stirring body opened.

"Morning, Gorgeous." His tongue tested his morning mouth.

"Merry Christmas, Ashton Walker."

"Merry Christmas to you too, Kristin Oakes."

"Well?" She brought her face inches from his.

"Well what?" He reopened his eyes, startled by her closeness.

"Are you ready to open presents?" She shivered with her excitement.

He rolled and glanced at the digital clock beside his pillow. "It's 5:12 a.m.. Are you five years old?" He raised his head to see her reaction to his inquiry.

"Come on! I can't wait." She pulled the pillow from beneath his head. "Santa's been here!"

"Santa? I told the HOA we needed security cameras and an intercom system to admit visitors into the building."

"You're such a putz!"

"You say that like it's a bad thing," and he brought his legs from beneath the bedding, locating his boxer shorts resting on the ebony ledge of the bed. He found himself waking in the nude quite often these days.

Once seated in one of the two living room chairs Ash was brought a small gift box by Krissy, now wearing a Santa hat with her nighttime T-shirt. He carefully unwrapped the foil paper, stalling for effect. He was met with a moan of frustration from across the living room. He pulled the paper away to find a cube-shaped wooden box, within it a stylish wooden watch.

"Wow! I've always looked at these watches in the catalogs on airplanes, but they're so outrageously expensive. You, you shouldn't have!" He took the watch from the box and held it up to study its workmanship. He stretched the band to slide over his wrist, then twisted to appreciate the design of the watch's face. "Wow…you shouldn't have."

"But I did," she giggled. "My turn." She searched under the tree to locate one of the two boxes she had seen labeled *To Krissy, From Ash*. The gift wrapping was far from professional with jagged edges and enough cellophane tape to secure a bank vault. Krissy stifled her reaction to laugh realizing this was probably his first attempt at wrapping a Christmas gift since the passing of his parents. She smiled her appreciation for his efforts.

Krissy made quick work of the paper with its geometric Christmas trees and shining stars. She opened the box to find another box within another box, each box wrapped in another floundering attempt at symmetry. The final box contained a keyring with several keys. She held the clinking pieces of brass up in search of an explanation.

"The keys are to the condo, the mailbox and the storage bin in the lower level. What was once just mine, is now yours too. It's just symbolic. I'm really not good at buying gifts."

She upped her appreciative smile. "I get it. I like it…It's just what I asked Santa for." She bound across the living room, sitting on his lap and slipped her tongue between his lips.

It was Ash's turn again. Krissy walked with a prima ballerina's gait as she pompously carried the bound together gift boxes. She passed the two festively wrapped shirt boxes, bundled together with a wide red ribbon to Ash, him giving

Chapter 16

A New Year, A New Challenge

With the arrival of the new year, Krissy Oakes initiated her first and only New Year's Resolution: Find a job, build a career.

Having met all of the residents of the top two floors with the creation of the stone soup recipe, she found a calling in assisting the seven elderly residents who remained relatively confined to the condominium building following the flood. The repairs from the break of the water main demanded more time than originally predicted. Access to the single elevator took almost four weeks due to parts being on back order. And the lobby was a hodgepodge of sawhorses and noxious odors as the contractors removed the nasty carpet and paneling, replacing it with ceramic tile and a white marble veneer. The slow shuffle of the elderly residents passing through the chaotic construction was strongly discouraged by the workmen just wanting to get the job done and without having to answer a dozen pointless questions while doing so.

Krissy had grocery shopped for those tenants of the seven upstairs units, carrying their purchases up the steps of the fire escape. She accepted checks, loose change and an occasional copy of a weekly entertainment magazine in payment for a half gallon of milk or a box of high fiber cereal. She'd meet delivery drivers in the lobby and would take larger grocery orders upstairs, making multiple trips dependent on the number of plastic bags left in the mailroom. Other deliveries from various local eateries were intercepted with the ordered meal delivered to the corresponding resident. Not to mention the daily delivery to each unit of the US Mail and the many pharmaceutical packages left on the shelf. Occasionally she'd even drive a package to the nearby residential hotel still housing the displaced first floor dwellers.

Every few evenings Krissy organize a nighttime bingo game, held in the alcove on each floor. She alternated the second floor one evening, the third floor the next evening. Ash even joined in on the evenings the event took place on their floor. Dining room chairs and TV trays were circled and Krissy called the numbers as the residents used their stashes of pennies to cover the numbers. Prizes were everything from quarters to cookies or brownies she had baked that morning.

On a Saturday afternoon, she sponsored a current events group, just discussing the events on the local news cast. Judy King hosted the second-floor group and Ashton Walker hosted the third-floor group. Krissy provided cookies for the participants as they debated the need for a new elementary school and the renovation of a wing in the art museum. The residents enjoyed their conversations and the connections they made with each other. Before each group ended their session a list of possible future activities was constructed, looking forward to the days when the residents were no longer homebound and could enjoy the surrounding neighborhood.

Krissy assumed the daily duty, no matter the weather, for taking *Emmitt* King, *Fido* Mueller, and *Spuds* McNeil for their morning and evening potty walks. Fido was a shih tzu mix and Spuds was an English bulldog mix. Ralph had agreed to keep Fido while Laverne resided in the extended stay hotel. None of the three dogs were pedigrees and each had their own distinct personalities. Ash attempted to help Krissy one evening by taking one of the more rambunctious pups on its leash but found himself covered in hives when the dog gave him a particularly wet lick.

"You really enjoy this, don't you?" Ash asked over dinner one evening as Krissy relived her day as the ad hoc director of senior services for the building.

"Yeah, I do. And I don't know why you don't like Doris. She's a real sweetheart."

"Eck," Ash writhed with his response. "Maybe you need to talk to Meredith and pool your talents. She reaches out to women learning to be independent and you reach out to people, people…"

"Needing other people." She sang the line from the Broadway musical.

"Yeah. Maybe you could form a service for shut-ins, to keep them active and connected. Don't most old folk's homes have an activity director? Maybe you could become one of those? Do they need special training? You've got experience! I'll even write you a reference!" Ash took his empty plate back into the narrow kitchen.

"I'll have to think about that... I told Corinne we were going to begin the search in Camdenton this Thursday and Friday for her siblings. She said she still hasn't received her results from the DNA test kit." Krissy buttered the dinner roll she took from the basket on the table. "It's too bad it's winter. I'd love to take a boat ride around the lake while we're so close."

"I, for one, am glad it is winter. A fireplace, a good glass of wine, a waiting bed..." Ash placed a kiss on the top of Krissy's head as he returned to the dining room table with a second helping on his plate.

"Ahem! Remember the purpose of this trip...And, you haven't seen the place where we're staying yet." She lifted her chin in warning.

"I'm sure we'll have time for a little *recreation* no matter where we stay." He paused to plan his attack on his full plate.

Ash and Krissy left for Camdenton, Missouri early that Thursday morning, the sun barely up. Ash struggled to carry his single duffle on top of one of Krissy's two suitcases as he traversed the matted carpet to the second-floor elevator, back in use. Krissy followed behind pulling her other suitcase and a backpack slung over her shoulder.

"Why do you need two suitcases for three days? We're coming home right after breakfast on Sunday. You really need to learn how to travel lighter."

"You'll see," came in warning.

"Whatever... I called the recorder of deeds in Camden County yesterday to give them a heads up we were coming and the reason for our visit. He was accommodating but said we might want to rethink our trip. He told me the county courthouse had a massive fire about fifty-five years ago and the old paper records served as kindling. He doesn't know how much or just what was salvaged."

"Dang! The probability of that was in the back of my mind."

"He said he'd try to snoop around and see what he could find if he got a chance before we arrived. He did suggest we still come down and perhaps talk to a couple of the older residents to see what they can remember." With the car trunk full, Ash turned on the sedan's signal and made the turn from the condominium's property in response to the voice on his GPS. "The guy said there's a few farmers who congregate in a local diner in the mornings. He said they're there almost daily since they're all retired and they've got nothing else to do."

The highway passed beneath their car as the map on Ash's cell phone directed them to the entry of the Prince Edward Motel, straight out of the 1940s without even a single attempt at updating since its Grand Opening. He pulled off the pavement of the blue highway and onto the gravel of the motel's parking lot.

Ash peered through the windshield, looking at the weathered façade of the antiquated motor lodge.

"And I thought the condo's lobby was deplorable. What in God's creation were you thinking, booking a room in this place?" he groaned.

"The rooms are actually very nice…in the photographs. And it did get some good reviews on TripTips.com." Krissy gave her perky sales pitch.

"Those photos were probably taken in 1946 and the reviews were probably, *'Has a good hourly rate.'*" Ash coasted into the vacant parking space before the door marked OFFICE.

"Ye of little faith," Krissy taunted, opening the passenger door. They both looked to see the sedan covered in the dust of the loose gravel. Krissy took her finger and drew a heart on the quarter panel, an arrow passing through it. She added an "A+K" beneath the heart.

The office door had no more than opened a few inches when the couple heard the waiting desk clerk, "You must be the Walkers." They both secretly liked how the *merger* sounded. Ash wondered if was way too early in their relationship to give it further consideration. He took a stealthy glance at Krissy, trying to glean her reaction, but she had turned away, moving towards the rack of brochures for local attractions. He thought he saw a robust pinkness in her cheeks when she took a quick peek back over her shoulder at him.

"Yes, I'm Ashton Walker. This is the little woman." He teased Krissy with a nose wrinkle when she again stood at his side. He heard her excitedly whisper, *"You're going to like what's in my suitcases."*

Ash, accustomed to hotel room cards that released door locks with a swipe, carried the large oval disc with the brass key attached. An embossed #14 was on one side of the plastic oval, but the artificial gold leaf had flaked off over the 4, leaving just an indentation. They began their walk down the chipped-up sidewalk connecting the rooms for the seedy motel. Picture window, sun-bleached red door, picture window, sun-bleached red door, picture window, sun-bleached red... all the way to room #14. The couple reached the dead red door with the brass numbers nailed at eye level.

"Here we are." Ash gave a dramatic shudder, then narrowed his eyes at the lovely woman beside him. "We'll enter, become immediately repulsed, and then we'll go look for the closest five-star hotel on the Lake."

"I tell you what. You go ahead in and give me about ten minutes. I'll bring the car down to the room." Krissy turned on the toes of her checkered high-tops and sprinted off towards Ash's car. A beat-up pickup truck was in the process of parking next to it.

Ash opened the heavy door and entered the room, smelling the distinct odor of mildew from the HVAC unit visible on the wall beneath the picture window.

The unit exhibited the brush strokes of numerous paintings over the decades, the irregular hum of the motor confirmed it was struggling to up the temperature of the motel room with its glossy cinderblock walls. The room's temperature matched the winter chill occurring on the other side of the single door.

Ash looked to see two queen-size beds with matching chenille bedspreads, dingy from age and a multitude of washings. A small television rested on the battered maple dresser. The brass pull for one of the dresser drawers dangled downward, one of its two screws missing. Ash debated leaving the key on the dresser and going in search of Krissy, making an immediate and unannounced departure from the slum.

He looked to the far end of the room to see his reflection in the large mirror above the counter containing the single bathroom sink. The silver on the mirror's backside was missing in patches around its border. Ash entered the bathroom to see seafoam green ceramic tile, coordinating with the bathtub to his right. A toilet in a smaller room was to his left. Even the Formica countertop of the vanity was in seafoam green with the white boomerang pattern, stylish in the year of its birth.

Ash pondered how to delicately tell Krissy there was no way he was going to spend the weekend in the seedy motel room that had probably entertained truckers and one-night stands for decades. After all, he was a professional, he was an attorney. The lowest he'd succumb to would be a budget level franchise hotel. He had standards! Had Krissy lost her pampered mind?

Ash heard knuckles deliberately knocking on the motel room's door. Tossing the oval keyring on the first bed, he opened the door to see a female figure. Her hair, a platinum blonde wig, was falling into her eyes cloaked by black framed sunglasses. She was wearing a canary yellow rain slicker barely reaching her thighs in black fishnet stockings. He looked down to see a pair of black and white checkered high-tops on her feet.

"You called for room service?" Luring, arousing...kinky.

He gave a snort. "Now I know why you brought two suitcases."

She brought her polished fingernails to his chest and forcefully pushed Ashton Walker back into the sordid motel room. Her voice went low and seductively airy. "Just go with it baby."

He also knew why she had booked them in the cringeworthy Prince Edward Motel. The sleazy motel room served to perfectly set the scene for her fantasy and for his every dream to come true.

"Ah yeah...yeah...Room service, right? I'd like a BLT with a side of coleslaw. Do you have Diet Mountain Dew?" he ineptly attempted to improvise.

"You're hopeless," was accompanied with rolling eyes. She immediately resumed her character. She removed the slicker to reveal her bare slender body save the fishnets secured by a black garter belt. Her nipples, protruding from the chill of the surrounding temperature, were shoved into his chest as she backed him towards the first queen size bed. Ash's eye devoured her beauty and he felt her hand go in search of the fly to his pants.

And so it began. Ashton Walker found himself the recipient of sexual favors he had only viewed on his laptop during lonely nights in his condo. He experienced tantalizing touches and firm caresses, and he reciprocated with techniques he never could see himself performing on any woman no matter how much he was falling in love with her... But he did.

Following the living out of the fantasy, Ash and Krissy navigated the downtrodden motel room, sharing a fast shower. They redressed and headed for the Camden County Courthouse. Ash was caught giving fleeting glances at Krissy in the passenger seat, a satisfied smile on his lips the entire ride to the courthouse. They were met by a security guard seated at the card table in the courthouse's lobby, him running a security wand over the two of them and directing them to the second-floor office of the recorder of deeds.

"You must be the guy from Kansas City." The man in his khakis and striped shirt almost bolted out the door of his office when he heard Ash speaking to the receptionist. "I'm Bob Boswell. We spoke on the phone." Visitors were obviously a rarity, the man desperate for a conversation with a fellow human being, preferably someone with news from the world outside of Camdenton, Missouri.

"Yes, Ashton Walker. This is my...my associate Kristen Oakes." *My associate? Hmm. Maybe he could counter with a fantasy or two of his own in their motel room tonight.*

"Well, I spent a little time yesterday afternoon looking up those names you gave me and I didn't have much luck. A couple of Collins surfaced, but their lines went in different directions. Most were people from St. Louis or Kansas City, just thinking they'd like life in the country and then booked when they found out that there's snakes and polecats around here and not much of anything else."

"You said some of the local residents might have memories of the family. Is there any way you can connect us to any of them?"

The receptionist raised her head from the word-find booklet open before her, looking up from a heavily marked-up page indicating she was a pro at the skill. "Melba Whitfield. She's ancient and she's always had her nose in everyone's business." Her head lowered and she went back to the puzzle in progress.

"Yep! Melba is your girl! She lives in the nursing home about four miles outta town from here. You had lunch yet? Fancy Nancy's is a good greasy spoon on your way there. That group of gossipy townsfolk I told you about hang out there. You can't miss them, they won't let ya. They'll be the ones all up in your business, wantin' to know who you are and what brought you to Camdenton."

Lunch did sound good to them. Seems the round in one of the queen-size beds of Room #14 had brought on hunger pains in the couple. They thanked the recorder of deeds, him telling them to just mention his name for a reference at the old folks' home. He added the fact he'd do them one better and call the place right now to tell them to expect visitors.

Ash and Krissy sat in a booth at Fancy Nancy's, perusing the single sided menu. It appeared the gossipy group was taking a day off to let their jaws recuperate. There were only a couple of other diners, them sitting by themselves at separate tables, in the culinary dive.

"So, what other kinds of costumes did you bring?" Ash's eyes were dancing in anticipation as he replaced the menu in its slot behind the chrome napkin dispenser.

"That's for me to know and you to find out." Her tongue did that lecherous glide over her lower lip.

"Can't wait… Pot roast sounds good. It's damn cold today. I hope we don't have to drive home in snow Sunday."

Ash and Krissy ate in relative silence. The single waitress puttered, filling the salt and pepper shakers behind the customer counter, along with taking unapologetic ganders at the couple. She would take turns, staring first at Ash and then at Krissy. Krissy returned one of her gawks to which the waitress gave a snarl of her upper lip. She drawled, "You ain't from around here, are you?" Krissy replied, "No, thank God" loud enough for only Ash's ears,

With the homestyle lunch completed, they drove the two additional miles to The Redeemer Senior Home. Ash speculated the facility's name came from the grim reaper waiting outside the building in wait to redeem the residents' souls. They pulled into a parking space on the lot before the sprawling single floor facility. A few rocking chairs sat unoccupied on both sides of the front door.

Walking from the parking lot Ash passed off the job of introductions and explanations to his assistant. "Since you're so good with the old people in our building, I'll let you do the talking with, with . . . What was her name?"

"Mel-ba Whit-field. No problem. If Melba's anything like Doris Pitman, you'd probably just end up snatching the old lady's oxygen tubes and watching her turn blue. I still don't know why you hate Doris so much. I get along fine with her."

"Maybe Doris hates men. I know she hates me." Ash reached for the handicapped push plate by the entry door of the home.

"You're projecting your own insecurity. She does not hate you."

Ash and Krissy passed through the double door entryway of The Redeemer Senior Home. A woman, no spring chicken herself, wearing a simple floral print dress and comfortable shoes stood waiting for them just inside the second set of doors.

"Mr. and Mrs. Walker?" *There it was again!* Ash wondered if a third time was going to be the charm? If they heard the merger announced a third time today, would it make the dream come true?

"I'm Ashton Walker. My partner, Kristin Oakes." Krissy duly noted her promotion from associate to partner.

"Bob called a little while ago and told me you were coming… I'm sorry to tell you that, that Mrs. Whitfield passed in her sleep last night." The woman brought her fist to her mouth, either to stop a release of emotions or prevent the revealing of additional confidential details. But no matter, the information that the couple had come in search of was now secured for eternity, unattainable to anyone.

"Son of a…" Krissy spun on the heels of her checkered high-tops and marched off, in the direction of the home's empty dining room. Her profanity laced rant was overheard as nothing more than a garbled drone left as a contrail of her forward motion.

"Don't mind her. We're just working on a case that she's taken to heart." Ash felt a sense of comradery with Krissy's display of humanism. Maybe money wasn't always the root of all evil, darkening hearts and supporting self-service. "Is there anyone else in the home who would know of a Collins family that lived in this area, at least fifty years ago?"

"Collins? Grady Collins?" Ash heard the shaky voice of an elderly man. He turned to see a shriveled figure seated in one of the recliners of the home's lobby. The back of the mans aged hand separated his chin from the knob of his cane. He looked up at Ash from behind coke bottle lenses, a luster coming to his face that had been disengaged just moments before..

"Yes! Yes sir! Grady, and a Horace Collins. A Corinne and a Cloris Collins. Do you recognize any of those names?"

"Nope, nope can't say that I do other than Grady. But then again, I have to look at my driver's license to even recall my own name these days." The two men laughed at the senior's sense of humor, still very much intact.

Ash called to Krissy, across the lobby, to rejoin him. Sensing the urgency in his voice, she bounded across the buffed floor. Ash had already begun to provide the elderly gent a succinct synopsis of the reason for the visit of the attorney and the bombshell to the old folks' home in Camdenton, Missouri. The elderly man introduced himself as Riley Hargrove, not taking his wallet out of his trousers to verify the fact. He said he had been a grade school classmate of a Grady Collins, probably seventy years ago, at least according to his questionable calculations.

"My brain functions about as well as a motor running on pond scum these days," he began. "But I do remember Grady. We was good buddies back then... Nobody on this earth deserved the sorrow he was subjected to. His family was dirt poor, his daddy a worthless grifter. His momma would spread her legs for... Sorry, ma'am," he apologized to Krissy with two fingers brought to his forehead in a salute to the lady..

The threesome spoke in the lobby of the nursing home for just over an hour. Ash retrieved one of his PaseoParkTechnology business cards from his wallet, handing it to the octogenarian. He wrote Riley Hargrove's personal information on the back of another card. He hoped his memory could hold all of details Mr. Hargrove had retold or at least Krissy could fill in the blanks. He looked forward to asking Corinne to verify the strength of the old man's testimony, confirming incidents and events. At least they had found some answers for Corinne. *Some* answers were so much better than the *none* she currently had.

Ash and Krissy learned things from Mr. Hargrove, things they questioned as to how to present to Corinne when they reported their findings to her. The man had consistently referred to Corinne's mother as a *floozy*. In current vernacular *whore* would be the more precise descriptor. Mr. Hargrove was amazed that three of the children even had the same last name of *Collins*. He speculated Corinne had more than five siblings. He even suggested Ash and Krissy expand their search into surrounding counties, looking for a man known to have had frequent rendezvous with the *floozy*. He couldn't recall the man's last name. *"It started with a T, or a P? Maybe a Z?"* Never mind the man had a first name. That name had been lost to Mr. Hargrove's dementia years ago.

Ash took a couple hours away from his desk the following Tuesday, arriving at the condo as Corinne Collins finished cleaning the master bathroom. He and Krissy sat at the dining room table with the woman, a bottle of beer open before her even in the morning hours. They took turns tactfully relaying their findings, revealing her mother's escapades tempered with the fact they were the foggy recounting of an old man just glad to have someone listen to his stories.

Corinne sat in her usual posture at the table, her eyes cast downward and her shoulders rounded. She sat silent for a moment at the conclusion of their report. She rose from the table, taking the empty beer bottle to the trash container in Ash's kitchen. Her disappointment was detectable as she thanked them for their time and efforts, her hearing nothing that she hadn't already sequestered in her memory. And then the woman returned to dust mopping the hardwood floors, softly singing a mournful hymn to herself.

Ash stood at the door to his apartment, Krissy readied to close the door behind him as he returned to his office. He got a twisted smile as he leaned in for a departing kiss.

"Why that smile?" she questioned.

"I feel like I should be thanking Corinne."

"For what?"

"For providing an opportunity for your performances as a call girl, a nurse, and a prison guard."

It was the same smile that graced his face as they checked out of the Prince Edward Motel in Camdenton, Missouri..

Chapter 17

Making Nice

Ash heard the rapping of knuckles on the glass of his office door. He called out, "Come in," expecting it to be a routine visit by Matt Blaylock. He looked up from the latest issue of the KCU Alumni magazine and into the face of Bernard Oakes, CFO.

"Mr. Oakes." He closed the magazine, attempting to slide it under a few waiting briefs.

"Bernie," he corrected. It seemed to cause the man some pain for him to offer this nicety. He again looked down at the leather tassels on his loafers. "Hillary and I are going to Chicago for the weekend with a few of the other couples from the top floor." He was referring to the spouses or love interests of the corporate executives for PaseoParkTechnology. "Perhaps you and Krissy would like to join us. The women can do their shopping thing and you can meet some people...make some connections. You know..."

Ash squelched his immediate response to the invitation. Instead of "*I'd hate nothing more*" came his fabricated, "I'd like nothing more. Thank you for the invitation."

A few logistics were worked out including their inclusion on the chartered jet with two other bigwigs and their tagalongs. Bernie left Ash's office stating his people would get ahold of Ash's people, those being Hilly and Krissy, and the balance of the minutia would be worked out. *Yahoo, ad sarcasm.* Ash slouched downward in his desk chair as he watch the backside of Bernard Oakes strut through the legal department and towards the bank of elevators.

The doors of the elevator had just closed, Bernard Oakes beginning his journey upwards, when the door to Ash's office was again flung open. With a quick toss, the KCU Alumni magazine now resided in the trashcan next to his desk.

"So buddy, what was that all about?" Matt asked, flopping into the barrel-back chair he always sat in during his interrogations of the witness.

"Nothing. Trust me, I'm going to do everything in my power to weasel out of it." Ash took a pen from the trough in his desk drawer and started to write on the notepad situated on his desktop. He purposely kept his eyes from Matt's, hoping Matt would take a hint and return to his own office. But he knew Matt would not leave it at that. Ash had no choice but to reveal the unsolicited invitation.

Matt made no attempt to mask his growing jealousy at the conclusion of the tale. "Like I said, it's not who you know... It's who YOU blow."

The term *blow* resurrected a pleasant memory from the Prince Edward Motel in Camdenton, Missouri and an unappreciative reaction to Matt's twisted perception of the purpose of the Chicago trip invitation. *But wasn't that exactly what was going to occur in Chicago, Illinois, Ash's sucking up to and kissing the behinds of the eighth-floor executives? Making those connections he had no desire or interest in.*

Ash and Krissy walked to the nearby Italian restaurant in the cold February air for dinner that evening. Over their pasta and red wine, Ash sought counsel on how to escape the weekend in Chicago. But Hillary had already called Krissy and the weekend's agenda was already under construction.

"Oh, Ash! It's been so long since Hilly and I have had a girl's day out, shopping and lunch, and on the Magnificent Mile. How much fun would that be!"

"Then why don't you go? Tell Bernie I have syphilis or chlamydia, or some other godawful plague, and I'm being quarantined."

She brought her wine glass upwards and focused on Ash with that unnerving stare of hers that never failed to garner his full attention. "STDs don't scare those jackasses. Oh Ash, that same group of infidels have refillable prescriptions for penicillin." She returned the goblet to the tabletop, and she grasped the corners of the table, thrusting her face closer to his. "They don't care if their girlfriends get pregnant. Roe v. Wade doesn't mean a blasted thing to them. They've all got providers on retainer."

"Oh, just the fraternity I want to rush with." Ash sat back in the booth, trying to remember if he had ever felt so dejected before in his life.

"Let's go to Chicago . . ." There was the head tilt, the sensuous smile that got Kristen Oakes whatever she desired from Ashton Walker. "All you have to do is nurse your brandy, nod your head and go back into your glass office on Monday morning."

"I have to look at Matt's pouty face. I have to listen to his cheap shots."

"How about this?" Beneath the table, Ash felt the pointed toe of her leather boot lifting the cuff of his slacks and then follow his tibia upward. "Let's go to Chicago . . . and I'll put on the costume I didn't get to use in Camdenton . . ."

Hmm… What would she be in Chicago? A gangster? A nun? A baseball player? Somebody play the National Anthem! Ashton Walker's flag was about to reach full staff.

***

He had never flown in a Lear jet before. He had never stayed in a luxury suite of a five-star hotel in downtown Chicago before. And he had never enjoyed handcuffs and a riding crop wielded by an attractive woman in a mock Gestapo uniform ever before in his lifetime.

Monday morning, his satchel over his shoulder, Ash walked towards the front doors of PaseoParkTechnology from the parking lot of the company peons. Matt called to him as he locked his own sporty vanity car and moved swiftly to join Ash. Matt was just about to catch up to Ash when they both heard a voice coming from the direction of the executive's gated parking lot.

"Hey! Walker! Lunch at the Chophouse Friday. See you there."

Ashton Walker immediately felt every vital organ within his body go on shutdown. He found himself reluctant to look at Matt Blaylock's face, but unable to cease and desist. He mustered a brittle smile in an attempt to deny his knowledge of the speaker and his intent to accept the invitation, but he knew he was caught dirty. The lunch invitation had been issued by the CEO of PaseoParkTechnology, one of Ash's co-participants in the weekend of debauchery conducted in the glitzy hotel in downtown Chicago, Illinois. Ash had spent until 3 a.m., seated in the hotel lobby bar, ingratiating himself with the CEO with his insights into how other tech firms played the buy-out game.

Ash cleared his restricting throat. "Perhaps . . . Thank you for the invitation . . . sir," Ash called back. Once again, Ash said a prayer of thanks that his voice had remained steady, even sounding somewhat mature.

"Lunch at the Chophouse . . . Nice." Matt sneered between his clenched teeth.

"Hey, he was just being nice. He probably doesn't mean it."

"Just exactly what went on over your weekend?" Matt's voice transitioned, becoming high pitched and whiney. "Was it good for you? Did you have a cigarette afterwards?" He even fluttered his eyelashes at Ash.

Ash's forward movement came to an abrupt halt. "You know what, Matt? You really don't look good in that particular shade of green. Jealous much?"

"I think my shade of green is more respectable than the brown spot in the middle of your face." And Matt's strides lengthened, his speed increased, and he broke away from Ash's side.

Ashton Walker came to an arrested halt on the sidewalk before the formidable building that housed PaseoParkTechnology. He looked up the façade, beyond his sixth-floor office window and culminating with the gilded eighth floor of the executive offices.

"I used to like this place," was Ash's dispirited assessment.

The morning progressed. Neither Matt nor Ash made the effort to reconnect for their usual 10:30 coffee break in the cafeteria. As one of the law clerks exited his office, Ash asked her if she'd mind bringing him a cup of coffee, offering to buy her a cup in restitution for her time and effort. He didn't know if he really wanted the coffee or was just bound by the routine. No matter, a few minutes later the paper cup was delivered to his desk top and the $4 was in the clerk's pocket.

He sipped the beverage no different from any other day or any other pot made in the company's cafeteria, but today tasting like the urine of a camel. He took his buzzing cell phone from his desktop, seeing the caller identified as *Gorgeous*.

"Hey."

"Hey to you too, Ashton Walker. You sound a little down."

He relayed the CEO's invitation and Matt's reaction, Ash not even trying to mask his mild exhilaration from the invitation and his irritation with Matt's immature reaction. Conflicted feelings were nothing new, but none-the-less discomforting to the attorney. He preferred black and white to shades of gray. He sought consistency and routine, only finding the unpredictability of Krissy tolerable, usually because it ended with his sexual gratification.

"Sounds like you might need a visit from Fraulein Oakes this evening." She finished in her best German accent, "Haf you been very, very bad, mein friend?"

"It sure would seem that way." *Was that a goosestep he felt in his boxers?*

"Well I don't have the most joyous of tidings myself, thus this phone call. The DNA company contacted Corinne. They contaminated her sample, and they are sending her a new test kit at no charge. Here she's waited a whole six weeks and now she has to wait another six weeks. What a waste!"

"She's waited decades. What's six weeks? Maybe they'll put a rush on it since they are the ones that screwed it up. Maybe you'll even get your money back as a courtesy."

"Just the same. She wants to know *now*."

Neither one of them wanted to acknowledge the sudden passing of Mrs. Whitfield, the busybody resident of The Redeemer Senior Home on the night before they were to interview her regarding Corinne's family tree. But the unfortunate event was in the back of both of their minds. Sometimes time is truly of the essence. Time truly isn't infinite.

Ash's usual afternoon coffee break with Matt didn't happen today. There was no joint walk to their cars, recapping highlights and low points of their day. And Ash said a silent prayer requesting no one from the eighth floor would even recognize him as he walked to his car at the conclusion of his day. Things were getting out of his control, and he didn't like the direction they were going.

Chapter 18

Brand Spanking New Lobby

"It looks absolutely amazing!" Vi Fabick oozed as she stood next to Ash Walker in the renovated lobby of the condominium building.

"We need a Grand Reopening celebration," Ash suggested even with the lobby's renovation having been completed a couple of weeks prior and all the displaced residents once again residing in their restored apartments.

"The Social Director is already on it."

"I should have known." Ash gave an upward toss of his eyes.

Krissy Oakes had joined forces with Ash's sister, Meredith, to form a spinoff company. While Meredith's forte was housekeepers and housekeeping, Krissy specialized in in-home entertainment and stimulation for the elderly and shut-ins. She had people looking to supplement their income, visiting clients in their homes with craft projects and other diversions to not only stave off boredom and loneliness, but to learn new skills and build relationships.

With the help of Ash's legal skills, the two women transformed their business into a joint not-for-profit, serving the elderly, the disabled and the disenfranchised. They provided employment opportunities for some and a life beyond just an existence for others. Even Hillary Oakes, Krissy's step aunt and sorority sister, used her Brighton College education and hoity-toity Kansas City connections to do fund raising. She was made responsible for branding and awareness through her constant postings on social media. The three ladies were a powerhouse of innovation.

Vi and Ash were joined by Krissy as she stepped from the once again functioning elevator.

"Greetings, sports fans!" she bellowed into the marble walled entry, making her voice boom even more. She leaned into Ash for his reciprocating kiss. "I found a portable bar through an events planner Hilly has used, and I got a deal on wine from a sommelier she has an ongoing contract with. Looks like the ribbon cutting is a go for next Friday evening. I will deliver invitations to everyone tomorrow morning."

"I found easy appetizers at Price King. Just heat and serve," Vi contributed.

"I guess I'm the bartender and the designated driver for the evening." The two ladies looked at Ash with questioning ganders. "Somebody has to push Esther's wheelchair to her door at the end of the party."

"True dat." Vi gave her signature shove to Ash's shoulder.

With Krissy's time consumed by her growing business, Ash returned to the kitchen and assisted with evening dinner preparation. The condo's kitchen being as petite as it was required one to cook and one to set the table. Ash, serving as sous chef, took the ingredients for a salad to the dining room table along with a cutting board and knife and began working on its assembly.

Krissy stood in the open doorway of the kitchen. She studied Ash with his attention focused on the wooden bowl of lettuce. "You're quiet tonight."

"It is what it is." He sliced the tomato, adding the rounds to the bowl.

"Matt still snubbing you?"

"Yeah. And it doesn't help when the head of the Legal Department starts playing favorites. We had a department meeting this morning, and Lou kept asking my opinion before anyone else could interject. He even offered me a cushy trip to settle a merger with a company that has already rolled over to play dead in Miami. Lou says, 'Why don't you take your girlfriend with you?' Jeez! Can he be a bigger butt kisser?"

"I'm sorry... You probably don't want to hear this, but Hilly said the same Chicago group is planning a retreat in Grand Cayman this summer. She said our names are at the top of the guest list."

"You can go without me."

"I'd never do that... I love you."

The couple froze, Krissy in the kitchen, Ash at the nearby dining room table. They had known each other five months, lived together four months, and this was a first. It was the first time the "L" word was used, spoken aloud, shared with the other. *No. No. Krissy had said early on that she thought she could love him, someday. Had that someday arrived?*

"I love you too," he said softly. Somehow his pity party seemed even shallower, more insignificant with this revelation. "I've loved you since the day we were introduced."

"I know… I just didn't want to look over enamored with you and scare you away."

"So is that why you told me about Bullocks and, and Go-Nads, and those other team mascots?"

She wove her arms around Ash's waist. "When I saw you blushing, I knew you were the guy for me."

The week passed and the grand reopening gala in the lobby of the condominium was underway. The white marble walls reflected the vivid lighting of the overhead canned lights with their moneysaving LED bulbs. The newly designed lobby had a crisp and modern look to enhance the building's first impression by visitors. The recently delivered furniture of black Naugahyde chairs and chrome tables was augmented that evening with dining room chairs from a couple of first floor units.

Vi Fabick's grandson, barely twenty-one, relieved Ash of his duty as the bartender so Ash could fully enjoy the party. The young man provided residents their choice of red or white wine served in souvenir wine glasses Hillary had designed. She created a new Parc LeMay logo, and it was engraved on each glass along with the date of the affair. Even Emmitt, Spuds, and Fido were in attendance, tethered on their leashes and strategically spaced in separate corners of the room. Commemorative water bowls were given to each pup, Hilly having painted their names on the black plastic bowls.

The party could only be described as a stellar success. Ash didn't even let Doris Pitman's remark that "all the white marble of the new lobby made the place resemble a mausoleum, just without plaques on the wall to denote which crypt belonged to which resident" get to him. Biting his tongue, he shared with Krissy, "Doris' plaque should be on the door to the trash shoot." To which he received Krissy's usual, "Be nice, Ashton Walker."

The residents mingled, comparing notes as to how they maintained their sanity during their isolation, during the month and a half the incapacitated elevator and ongoing construction forced them to stay on their respective floor. Ash likened it to a reunion of war veterans, comparing battle stories and showing off resulting scars. He marveled at how Krissy had taken on the opportunity, focusing on others and allowing her to grow as a person. It brought out the beauty within her, now matched to the physical beauty she consistently projected.

Vi Fabick's strong voice was heard over the ten jovial voices and the three growling dogs. "Ladies and gentlemen, your attention please! I would like to take this opportunity to extend our thanks to Ash and Krissy for getting us through the rough spots. They kept us fed and entertained, and for that we thank them."

A round of "hear, hears" and applause followed, drawing a blush from Ash and a small curtsy from Krissy. "Our pleasure, but it was really all Krissy's idea and doing. I just did as I was told," replied Ash as he pulled her into his side.

The party continued as the wine flowed and the guests continued to mingle. The room of thirteen revelers began to fall silent and all eyes turned to see the consistently disheveled woman standing in the lobby's front door.

"Oh, oh… I'm, I'm sorry. I didn't mean to interrupt your party," she stammered. Her eyes skimmed face to face, her looking all-the-more horrified at her intrusion.

"It's okay, Corinne. You probably know everyone. Come on in," Ash called to the woman nervously tugging at her heavy cardigan.

"Have a drink, Corinne. You *should* be part of this celebration as often as you are here. You must love this new lobby without that nasty old carpet." Vi Fabick followed Ash's lead, including the woman and attempting to alleviate her obvious discomfort.

"I…I just had something to show Ash and Krissy, but I guess it can wait."

Krissy spied the envelope in Corinne's hand, the logo of the DNA testing firm as the return address.

"You got your results! What did you find out?" Krissy placed her wine on the end table and lurched upwards towards the woman in her excitement.

The envelope was protectively drawn into the woman's chest. "I, I haven't opened it yet. I...I didn't want to be alone to read that...that they couldn't find nobody." Her eyes flashed again around those gathered in the lobby.

Ash soothingly raised his open palm to calm the woman. "Corinne, may I explain to everyone what's going on here?"

With Corinne's permission, Ash stopped the festivities to explain the situation to the people now silent in the lobby. The other residents knew nothing about the toy monkey and its malfunctioning cymbals, about Ash and Krissy's trip to Camdenton, or their conversation with Mr. Hargrove in the lobby of The Redeemer Senior Home. They listened respectfully as Ash relayed the events, the dignity and feelings of Corrine Collins protected by the lawyer.

"You're among friends here, Corinne." Krissy moved beside the woman. "We're all here for you no matter what you find out in that letter."

"Thank you, I appreciate that . . . but . . ." *But, you aren't family. You aren't blood.*

Corrine Collins methodically slipped her fractured fingernail beneath the flap of the envelope. She did that see-saw motion, ripping the paper, and then pulling out the folded letter. She opened it barely reading the introductory paragraph and going straight to the seven names listed below it. She skimmed the names, going immediately to their level of relationship. A second cousin, a great-great aunt, an uncle...a sister...A half-sister to be exact.

"I... I got a sister . . . well, a half-sister. But I'll take her! She's family! We're related." The woman fought back her tears, but the smile was uncontrollable.

Krissy reached for the letter, "May I see it?"

Krissy, too, went immediately to the list of names. None were familiar, none were making a significant impression until she came to the name of the half-sister.

"Oh, my God!" Krissy looked directly at Ash, and then she turned to look at the woman who lived across the hall in 3D. "Doris...you may have a half-sister too."

"What? What are you talking about?" the woman blurted. Her bewildered eyes darted from guest to guest.

Ash removed the letter from Krissy's hand and did his own reading. "Doris, did you ever do one of those ancestry tests? You know, a DNA test to see where your family came from?" asked Ash, moving towards his nemesis.

"I...I did a few years ago." In a semi-controlled flop, she lowered her aged body into one of the new Naugahyde chairs.

It was Krissy's turn to question the person on the stand. "What were your results? Do you remember? Do you still have them?"

"I never opened the letter either. I put the envelope in a scrapbook, and I just forgot about it... I didn't want to be disappointed. I was accustomed to being alone and I didn't want to find out that I really was...all alone."

"Do you still have the letter? You said you put it in a scrapbook?" Ash questioned.

"Yeah. I put it in the scrapbook with my 4-H stuff." Doris looked to Krissy. "You know, the one I showed you when you wasn't grounded anymore." Ash was met with a chiding grin, reconnecting him to the time when he forbid Krissy to leave their condo, fearing Bernard Oakes's vengeful wrath. "Run up to my place, Krissy. It ain't locked. Find the letter and bring it down here."

Meanwhile, Corinne moved to the side of Doris Pitman, pointing where the letter listed her name. Doris studied the typed correspondence. Krissy returned to the lobby, finding Doris still in the Naugahyde chair, Corinne now seated in a dining chair next to her. The two women sat with their hands joined together as if Doris and Corrine were the last two candidates in a Miss America Pageant, one waiting to be named the runner up, the other the new Miss America.

"You open it, Krissy. My hands are shaking too bad," directed Doris.

Krissy made quick work of the envelope, withdrawing the letter. She passed the folded document to Doris. All the occupants of the lobby stood crowded around the two women seated side-by-side. Doris pulled her reading glasses from the top of her head, and she too skipped the intro paragraph, going straight to the list of five family matches.

"No...no... Corinne isn't listed." Her voice exposed her disappointment with the lack of a connection. A silent sadness depleted what remained of the festive atmosphere of the party.

Ash cried out, "She wouldn't be! You took the test before she did! She wasn't in the bank of results! Doris! You need to take the test again and if it's a match with the latest bank, Corinne should show up as your half-sister too." There was a cheerful outburst and the party regained its energy.

"That probably isn't really necessary," Jerry Kaplan, 2A, quietly shared.

"What Jerry? What did you say?" asked another resident.

His aged eyes brightened. "Look at their faces. They're shaped the same, high foreheads, broad cheekbones. Even the shape of their noses, that little bump at the bridge." He made an attempt at pointing to their noses, his palsy making the direction hard to follow.

"I see it!" agreed Gwen Adams, 1A. "Their cheekbones are the same. Kind of high."

"Do you remember a Grady or a Horace?" Corinne asked Doris.

Doris got a faraway look as she searched her own faulty memory. "Horace? Horace?" Her eyes brightened. "He couldn't say Doris, so he'd called me Cloris. I'd remember him whenever I'd see Cloris Leachman on the TV."

Ash recalled Cloris as one of the possible names he took with him on the jaunt to Camdenton, the trip originally thought to be an unsuccessful waste of time. Little did he know then, the old codger at the nursing home was providing a valuable link to solving the case. Ash had a sudden fleeting visual of Krissy in the platinum wig and yellow rain slicker at their motel room's door, nothing on underneath . . . *Maybe later tonight.*

Ash did a comparison of the two letters finding that the names listed consistently matched between the ancestry banks. Doris and Corinne were indeed related. Neither woman was going to bed that evening feeling alone in the world. They now had each other.

The party broke up. Thank yous were once again bestowed on Ash and Krissy. The bar was packed up and the lobby restored to its pristine order. The residents returned to their respective units. And Corinne Collins spent the night with her half sister, Doris Pitman of 3D, reminiscing and filling in missing memories until the early morning hours.

Chapter 19

The Parting of Ways

Ashton Walker drove to his office that Monday morning with a smile on his face the entire way. He kept replaying scenes from the reopening gala and the announcement that Doris and Corinne were half-sisters. That was until he pulled into a parking spot and Matt Blaylock pulled into the spot next to him. His smile immediately disintegrated. He got out of his car, pulling the leather satchel across the center console. No good morning, no acknowledgment passed between the two former friends. He could no longer take Matt's cold, detached attitude. "This is ridiculous!" Ash all but shouted.

"Is it?" Matt stopped, turning his torso to give Ash his full attention. "Senior counsel. Senior counsel! We started here three weeks apart, me before you. I went to a ranked law school, and you, you went to a lowly public school of law and . . . and cosmetology. And *who's* named the new senior counsel for PaseoParkTechnology? Yeah, it's beyond ridiculous."

"I agree. It's ludicrous. I didn't ask for the promotion."

"But you took it."

Ash lost his patience with Matt Blaylock. "You're right, Matt. It's not who you know, but who you blow. Maybe you should stop blowing your horn and let someone see you actually be productive and do something besides whine." He stood back and watched Matt proceed towards the front door of the firm, him giving an overzealous greeting to one of the cute young law clerks in her too tight sweater, too short skirt.

Ashton Walker sat at his desk waiting for his blood pressure to return to a healthy level. Counting to one hundred didn't even phase the current level of anger coursing through his veins. Yeah, he did. He took the title of senior counsel with the substantial pay increase. But he asked to retain his smaller office in an attempt to maintain his humility. Perhaps it was more of an attempt to placate the expected hurt feelings and bruised ego of Matt Blaylock.

Well, that failed, too.

***

"You look drop-dead gorgeous tonight. But then again, you usually do." Ash brought Krissy's hand upwards to bestow a kiss on her soft knuckles. He wondered why he hadn't placed a ring on her finger yet. How long had they known each other? Six months lived together almost five. Too soon?

"You don't look so shabby yourself," she smiled back.

"Well, let's go do this thing." He heaved a heavy sigh.

"Relax. Enjoy the gala. They can be a lot of fun and usually there's an open bar." Krissy said, trying to appease his apprehension.

"Fun? Easy for you to say. You know which fork to use when eating your soup."

"Goofball!" A snort escaped her slender nose.

Krissy entered the hotel ballroom on the arm of Ashton Walker. She was wearing a floor length designer gown in a pale shade of periwinkle. He was in a tailored tuxedo and black tie. He had gone ahead and purchased the dapper formalwear since this was his third black-tie event in less than two months. Once again he was representing PaseoParkTechnology at another charity gala. The rented tuxes for the other galas were ill-fitting, their cummerbund too taut and the suspenders digging into his shoulder blades during the evening. But not tonight. The skilled tailor had shrouded his mildly muscular build perfectly.

"Ashton! Krissy! Over here."

Ash glanced to his right, recognizing the gentleman rising from his chair and motioning for them to join his table. Howard Meyer, president of one of the large hospitals in Kansas City. Ash did a quick scan of the faces of the other six people already seated at the table. He recognized the CEO from another health care facility, an upper-level executive with a recognized financial firm and a retired state senator, all seated with their respective spouses. He had met each of them at other charitable affairs. As he passed between the surrounding tables Ash was met with acknowledgements from a couple of other guests, they too being executives from established Kansas City firms.

Following the Thanksgiving dinner in the home of Bernard Oakes, Ash had served as a frequent seat filler for a couple of the muckety-mucks of PaseoParkTechnology. Bernie told Ash to take advantage of those opportunities to schmooze, make new friends, and make those connections that could springboard him into a mahogany-paneled office on the eighth floor of PaseoParkTechnology before he was forty.

Ash continued to deny social climbing as a goal of his. He wasn't comfortable with the attitude and arrogance of those people in top management positions. No longer having lunch or coffee breaks with Matt Blaylock, he began to reluctantly join Bernie and the others with job titles beginning with a capital C for lunch. He had dined several times at the Chophouse, his lunch tab picked up on the corporation's credit card and his consistent offer to reimburse always refused. He sat having conversations with the CEO, the CFO, the COO, the CIO, and some other Cs he had absolutely no idea what their letters stood for or what the person actually did for the company.

There were other *things* consistent amongst all of those people whose title began with the letter C. These things began with the letter c, too. Champagne, caviar, cocaine and a speculated level of corruption. Perhaps no more or no less than within any other top tier company, but still unnerving to the lowly corporate lawyer.

Ash had overheard snippets of conversations not meant for his ears. Whispered discussions regarding stock dealings, padded expense accounts, even kickbacks. Once, while in a restroom stall, he recognized Bernie's gruff directive to manipulatively drive up the stock of a small-time competitor and then tank them in a few weeks, making them an easy target for PaseoParkTechnology's takeover.

Ash speculated that just maybe he should start getting his resume in order and begin looking elsewhere for employment... But they came looking for him first.

***

The telephone situated on the corner of Ash's desk began its buzz. Ash spit the depleted piece of chewing gum from his mouth into the trash can and put the receiver to his ear.

"Mergers and Acquisitions. This is Ashton Walker."

"Mr. Walker, you probably don't remember me, but about a six months ago you met with my father, my older brother and myself to walk us through the paperwork giving PaseoParkTechnology the right to pillage our family business in Seattle. I'm Doug Bryant. Bryant Technology was the company."

A knot began forming in the pit of Ash's stomach. Was the guy harboring growing anger, stalking him? Was he waiting outside the building with a gun? Mr. Bryant had every right to his anger. Ash had truly raped the small tech firm and robbed it blind...No, PaseoParkTechnology had royally screwed over the three family members. Ash was just the hired hit man. Instead of $2.4 million apiece, each family member should have been paid in the range of $4 million apiece. Additional restitution should have been given for a couple of patents, but it wasn't even mentioned. Ash remembered sitting in the tavern with the father and his two sons, none of the foursome having any appetite. The three Bryant men lost their hearts that day; Ash had lost his soul.

Ash swallowed and took a deep breath. "I, I remember you, Mr. Bryant. What can I do for you?" He debated signaling a law clerk to have the call traced by security.

"I'm starting a new tech firm. I've teamed up with a whizbang out of Poly and one out of an East Coast power school for technology. We just signed the lease today on a building in the Power and Light District of Kansas City. We like the idea of a Midwestern location for our headquarters... And I want to see PaseoParkTechnology brought to their knees and starved to death. We need a lawyer, and we want one who has scruples and character to take

PaseoParkTechnology down legitimately and honestly. Not like PaseoParkTechnology did to Bryant Technology."

Ash felt a lightheaded sensation taking over his brain. "Are you, are you referring to me or are you looking for a recommendation? Someone local?"

"Yes, you Mr. Walker. Your face was the same somber shade of gray as the three Bryant faces that day. You wear your heart on your sleeve, sir. You didn't want to be in that room signing those documents any more than my father, my brother, and I did. You have scruples… You just need to grow yourself a set of balls."

Well, I've got the T-shirt, Ash thought, suddenly envisioning the Paske Community College T-shirt Krissy had given him for Christmas, Go-Nads emblazoned across the chest. He wondered how the T-shirt would look beneath a suitcoat? How would he wear a necktie with it?

"I . . . I don't know what to say. I'm usually not at a loss for words, but frankly I've got nothing." Ash reclined in his desk chair.

"I'll tell you what, I'm going to be in Kansas City for a few days. Let's get together for lunch or a drink and I can show you what we have to offer. I know you're not the type to run back to your employer and spill the beans. Like I said, you've got scruples. And if you do, well I'll see you in court."

"Okay. I'll at least give you the courtesy of my consideration. No guarantees."

"That's all I ask for."

Ash floated through the remainder of his day. His thoughts were those of a ping-pong ball in a table tennis match, a tennis ball at Wimbledon, a volleyball in a game on a sandy beach, going from one side of the net to the other. PaseoParkTechnology versus Doug Bryant's new tech firm.

It was her fault, all Kristin Oakes's fault! If she had never come into his life, he would still be living with a comfortable routine, being friends with Matt, and retiring from PaseoParkTechnology as predicted on his hiring day by the faceless woman who no longer worked in HR. *Darn you, Krissy Oakes! Darn you woman!* But God, he loved her.

He parked his new luxury crossover in his slot in the lower-level parking garage of the condominium building. He rode the elevator to the third floor. Standing in the hallway before the door to 3C he heard the laughter of Doris Pitman and Corinne Collins through the closed door to Unit 3D. *At least someone had a happy ending to their fairy tale. Mine is just taking some unsolicited turns. Mine's not over yet.*

He had reached an agreement with himself during his elevator ride to the third floor. He would not mention the potential job offer to Krissy. *Why did she have to know? She wasn't his wife. Why wasn't she his wife? Jeez! Wasn't there already enough on his plate?*

It was Ash's night in the kitchen, Krissy's night to set the table and do the clean-up. He saw the table was already set, four place settings in position. He dropped his satchel to the floor and suppressed the groan building in his chest.

"We've got dinner guests tonight?" he sulked.

"Yeah, Bernie and Hilly. Remember?"

The deep sigh escaped, followed by, "Release the kraken."

He began searching for the necessary pots and pans to prepare tonight's menu. He took the package of four chicken breasts from the refrigerator, removing them from their packaging and staging them in the glass baking dish. Ash felt his apprehension building. He truly had no desire to talk to anyone over dinner, most assuredly, not Bernard Oakes. What if he let it slip that he was thinking about jumping ship? Even the slightest hint of his departure from PaseoParkTechnology would most likely cause the playing field to be reshuffled, with Ash returning to the position as a bench warmer. *Maybe that wasn't such a bad thing since he wasn't enjoying his current position. Hell, he might even be fired, brought up with charges, him suspected of corporate espionage!*

The evening went according to script. Krissy and Hilly vacillated between business and pleasure topics in their conversations. Occasionally they would make reference to the trip to Grand Cayman, coming up in just a few weeks. Listening to their banter, Ash repeated to himself his resolve to again pass on the cocaine, just as he had done in Chicago.

Bernie Oakes finished off the bottle of Kentucky bourbon Ash kept just for himself, specifically for nights like this one. Bernie was in one of his foul moods, even beyond his usual level of obnoxious this evening, crossing the border into downright repulsive. He made a lewd remark directed at Krissy and executed an outright grab at Hillary as she got up to help clear the table.

"That'll be enough, Bernie. That's not how women are treated in this house." Ash's voice was firm.

"Wimp." Bernie killed off the last of the bourbon in his glass.

An attack of paranoia took possession of Ash. Did Bernie know about the phone call from Doug Bryant? Had PaseoParkTechnology security tapped his office phone and shared the contents of the conversation with Bernie? Did Bernie know about the job offer or the scathing plan of the newly forming tech firm to obliterate, or at least greatly wound, PaseoParkTechnology? Is that why he was behaving like such a jerk tonight?

With Hillary and Krissy engrossed in a movie on the living room television, Bernie and Ash adjourned to the home office. Ash sat behind his desk, giving him a sense of superiority for a change over the inebriated CFO. He felt a limited sense of protection, knowing the piece of furniture could serve as temporary barrier from the drunk, allowing Ash a chance to escape in the event of a physical attack by the lush.

"Well, you're making a favorable impression on the eighth-floor honchos." Bernie, rocked back in the chair before the bookcase, skimming down the row of titles. "George Truex announced his plans to retire in two years…if he isn't forced out first. George isn't much of a team player these days. Hell, he's more of a slacker if you ask me." Bernie stood to look at Ash's diploma from Kansas City University School of Law. "Your name was tossed out as a possible replacement for George… Ashton Walker, Chief Operations Officer. You think you could be ready for the first string in two more years?" The imposing man turned to gage Ash's reaction.

"I'm flattered, but I also know I'm nowhere near ready for such a position now. I don't know that two years will even be sufficient for me to prepare for a position at that level."

"Well, keep doing what you are doing and you will be ready. Two years, if not sooner, should be enough time for a hot shot like you."

Ash couldn't resist testing the waters. "I'm not so sure I want to, to be an exec with PaseoParkTechnology."

"There's probably no better place in Kansas City, maybe the entire country to have a career at the top." Bernard Oakes reclined in the chair, his ankles crossed along with his arms above his puffed-out chest in a challenge to Ash's dispute of his claim. "There's a bonded network there and we watch out for each other's best interest."

Ash read between the lines, between Bernard Oakes' words. *They protect each other.* From what? No longer comfortable with the topic and the possibility of his inclusion in something he wanted no part of Ash changed the topic. He chose to talk about the local football team, the upcoming baseball season, the opening of a new burger joint near the office. Anything except discussing his waning allegiance to PaseoParkTechnology.

***

"You were awfully quiet at dinner tonight," Krissy said as she slipped off her bra, dropping it on the ebony shelf surrounding the king size bed. "Something wrong?"

"Nah, there's just a lot more on my plate with the new job level."

"Well, in just a few weeks we'll be basking on the beach of Rum Point, a piña colada in hand and not a care in the world."

Ash wondered how soon he would be allowed to take a vacation if he joined the new firm? *Then again he wouldn't be taking a trip with the head honchos of*

PaseoParkTechnology if he didn't work there any longer. His brain took a bounce to happier thoughts. He realized he could actually walk to the Power and Light District from the condo. It was a vibrant area, unlike the area surrounding the condo. *Should he look into moving just five blocks?* The volleyball match had resumed in his head. His mind wondered from topic to topic until he heard Krissy vomiting in the bathroom.

"Are you okay?" he called to her.

"I will be. I should have never eaten those artichoke hearts. They always make me puke."

"They were pretty gross. What was the expiration date on the can? Did you look?"

"They were from a new can...Bernie was pretty gross tonight too. That sexist joke of his wasn't at all funny . . . I wonder if he's cheating on Hilly? He better watch his back. She'll absolutely crucify him."

"I heard Corinne's voice over at Doris's. They've really clicked."

"Who would have ever thought?"

"Well, good night, Kristen Oakes."

"Good night, Ashton Walker."

At precisely 2:23 a.m., Ash experienced his own second coming of the artichoke hearts. He rose from his knees before the toilet and washed his mouth out at the sink. Looking at his reflection in the mirror he wondered if the artichoke hearts carried salmonella. Or could it just be the stress he felt from the phone call from Doug Bryant? More likely, he wondered if Bernie Oakes had slipped something into his iced tea at dinner and tried to poison him?...But Krissy was sick too? Bernie loved Krissy like his own daughter...The merry-go-round continued in his brain until he finally fell asleep.

Chapter 20

Making it Official

"Mr. Bryant, this is Ashton Walker" was how the phone call began.

Ash stopped by the administrative assistant in the Legal Department's desk, letting her know he would be taking an extended lunch today, giving the excuse that he had some personal business to take care of. *Well, he did.*

Ash straightened his tie and took a fast glance in the mirrored wall of the restaurant's lobby. He looked through the flimsy fabric of the room divider separating the dining room from the hotel, and he tried to remember what Doug Bryant looked like six months ago in Seattle. He zeroed in on a man with a receding hairline and comical oval glasses, him perusing the menu.

Ash stood before the vacant hostess desk thinking the hotel's restaurant was pretty *high on the hog* for someone starting a new business. But then again the somewhat experienced entrepreneur had recently come into $2.4 million, thanks to the takeover by PaseoParkTechnology. But if the new venture failed that $2.4 million would be the first thing to be gone. What was the saying? Go big, or go home? Is there any difference between going bankrupt for a dollar or for a million dollars? You were still bankrupt. The hostess interrupted Ash's scattered thoughts, confirming that the balding man was indeed Doug Bryant and he was waiting for an Ashton Walker.

The man rose from his chair as Ash approached the table with its long white tablecloth and stiff napkins. His hard stare began to relax into an amiable smile. His hand was extended in friendship.

"Good to see you Ash. Well at least it's more pleasant to see you this time compared to that last go around." Doug Bryant laughed nervously. He gestured for Ash to take the other chair. A waiter immediately attended the table, requesting a bar order from the two men.

"I'll have a Bloody Mary. Ash?"

"A gin and tonic, please."

The waiter disappeared and Ash picked up the hefty menu, opening it to find choice cuts of steaks listed with no prices. He surmised his lunch was going to be a business write-off just as his meals with the eight-floor executive always were. Somehow he was slightly more comfortable with the arrangement this time around.

"So, you're going to give technology another run." Ash hoped he hadn't sounded smug or belittling. Bryant Technology had been one of the better acquisitions PaseoParkTechnology had ever snagged, providing not only quality programs but utilizing streamlined production techniques, much more cost efficient than those currently in use. The Bryant family were experts at running a successful business.

"It's what I know. It's what I do best. My dad was just losing his momentum and not willing to listen to his snot nosed sons' suggestions... He died two months after we sold the company." Ash couldn't hide his horror at the coincidence and Doug couldn't stifle a vindictive grin in retaliation. "Don't beat yourself up. It wasn't your fault. He had cancer and didn't tell any of us."

"You know, I really don't need your attitude or arrogance. I've got a job and I'm looking at a lucrative future with PaseoParkTechnology." Ash heard the voice in the back of his head telling him to cool his heels and listen to what the man had to offer.

Doug brought a sizeable packet from his lap, passing it across the table to Ash "Take your time. Look this over. Questions? Ask. Comments? Make them."

Inside the manila envelope were the printouts of a PowerPoint presentation, organized within a glossy folder. It laid out the new venture's mission statement. Its marketing plan. Its financial investment plan. Its list of backers and the forming team roster. Most of the words and the numbers meant very little to Ash. He'd never even run a crew in a burger joint much less at a viable corporation. But a few names on the list of players and supporters caught his inexperienced eye.

He read the names of people already onboard with the new Bryant Technology 2.0. Ash recognized two particular names. Ash had sat across the table from both of them, Ash holding the straw and sucking the life out of their tech firms. Their well-managed companies with viable tech products and services had been major acquisition for PaseoParkTechnology. William Cole and Phil Zimmerman were now seated on the founding board of directors for the rebirth of Bryant Technology into Bryant Technology 2.0. Their expertise would be invaluable.

Doug Bryant spoke with not only passion but confidence regarding the venture. He had acquired sharp minds to create and to deliver the product. And he had established corporations and recognized companies poised to shift their loyalties from PaseoParkTechnology to Bryant Technology 2.0. Only time would tell if the *big boys* would really transfer their allegiance, or if they were just trying to placate the new guy sitting in their office and selling nothing more than a concept. If indeed they took their business to Bryant Technology 2.0, PaseoParkTechnology would most assuredly feel the slice of the knife and bleed profusely.

"Let me sleep on this for a night or two," Ash requested.

"Certainly. You may be sitting in a nice position with PaseoParkTechnology now, but you can be sitting on a throne with Bryant Technology 2.0. Head of Legal, has a nice sound to it, doesn't it?"

"I can't eat a title." Just like he couldn't eat COO, or any of the other capital C's at PaseoParkTechnology.

"But $255,000 annually, along with profit sharing and a stock option, will put a lot of groceries on your table."

"That it will."

Ash returned to his glass office, finding it next to impossible to focus on anything. He found himself going from document to document, not investing the energy necessary to make sound decisions or proposals. He'd just come back to them tomorrow when he'd have a cleared head and hopefully a decision rendered. He looked through his glass door and into that of Matt Blaylock, wishing they were still friends and he could be a sounding board for the dilemma raging in his head. But Matt would be the last one to learn of the job offer if he ever did hear about it.

Dinner that evening was in a Chinese restaurant at Krissy's request. She said their egg foo yong had been calling her name. Ash liked their beef with broccoli. He also like having her company, him no longer feeling inhibited by having to dine alone. He reached across the table and rested his hand on the top of hers, just as he had watched the couple on their double date at Vito's doing only months ago. He still found it hard to believe that Kristin Oakes was in love with him.

"I . . . I had lunch with a guy, not much older than me, today." Ash wondered why he felt the need to add the piece of personal trivia. Was Doug Bryant too young to be successful? "He's starting a new technology company right here in Kansas City. He wants to see PaseoParkTechnology on their knees and kissing his--"

"Like that'll ever happen." Krissy slipped the large spoon under the patty of fried egg, chicken and green onions, moving it to her plate then slathered it with brown gravy.

"With this guy," Ash said, raising his eyebrows in warning. "PaseoParkTechnology better be paying attention."

"You think he really has a snowball's chance in Hell?"

Ash used his tongue to remove the clump of rice in his gums. "He most definitely is going to be a force to be dealt with." He put his fork on his plate. He waited until Krissy's eyes were locked in the crosshairs of his. "He wants me to run their Legal Department. He wants me to be their Head of Legal."

"Jeez," she brought her own fork to her forehead, her eyes burning into him.

The couple went on to discuss the contents of the printed PowerPoint presentation. Ash shared the proposed annual salary, starting at $150,000 and increasing with every new client committed to Bryant Technology 2.0, the prospect of reaching $255,000 within a year, year and a half max . . . and the title, Head of Legal. *Take that, Matt Blaylock!*

"Well, it's your decision. I'm just along for the ride." She took another spoonful of sticky rice, adding it to what had already been dolloped onto her plate.

Ash tossed his dinner fork, it making that irritating clink as it landed on his china plate. "And what's that supposed to mean?"

Unphased by his fitful outburst she merely took the tepid pot of green tea, pouring first into his cup and then into hers. "Ash, I'm not married to you. I'm not your wife, a legal partner with a vested interest." The only thing missing was her usually sarcastic "ta da" at the end.

"You could be," he fired back, irritated with his own irritation. *Where did that tidbit come from? Just because he'd thought about popping the question on the car ride home from work he still hadn't.* What kept him from asking her? Was it the ten-year age gap? Is ten years too many? Had they not known each other long enough to make a sound decision? Seriously? They currently lived together! They'd never even had an official fight. Wasn't that a sign they were compatible? Were they having their first fight now?

She released a nervous laugh. "What says I'd even want to marry you, Ashton Walker?" There were those stunning gray-blue eyes, giving him the look that instantly stirred the sleeping beast in his nether regions.

"Well, think about it, Ms. Oakes. Let me know when you've reached your decision."

"Wow. That's quite the marriage proposal." She looked at him with disgust, shaking her soft, ash-blonde hair. "I better not answer the door tomorrow, or I might be met with a subpoena to appear before a judge so we can get married."

"I didn't mean it that way . . . No . . . If . . . When I propose to you, you'll be swept off your feet." He picked up his fork and resumed cutting the lengthy strip of beef into a few manageable pieces. He could feel his temper starting to subside.

"Well, that's exactly what I'm expecting to happen." She sat back for the waiter to refill her water glass, then took a lengthy swallow to quench her thirst and calm her own heightened emotions.

He cautiously asked, "Have you . . . considered it? Marriage?"

"Yeah." Cue the head toss, the look from the corner of her eyes. "But only with you, Ashton Walker. No one else but you."

The owner of the restaurant appeared at their table, making the usual inquiries regarding the quality of their food and the level of their service. The moment was lost, unable to be resurrected in its honesty and intensity. They both felt inwardly disappointed that the discussion had not come to a satisfactory resolution. Then again, neither of them considered Wan Fu Garden the best location for an over-the-top marriage proposal.

Ash held the door open for Krissy to exit the small restaurant. He hoped to resurrect the topic of marriage and renew their conversation, while maintaining an air of neutrality. As she passed him he questioned, "So, what would be some of your choices of music for our first dance if we did get married?"

"Hmm." She paused tapping her lips, then moved out of the way of the couple trying to enter the restaurant. "Maybe it's easier for me to say what are hard 'no's' for me. Nothing trendy and overworked. Nothing that demands great dancing skill or talent. And nothing that'll make me cry every time I hear it if you ever leave me."

"My God, Krissy! Why would I ever leave you?" He felt like he had been punched in the gut by a prize fighter. *So much for neutrality!*

She brought her arms around him and apologetically smiled into his wounded face. "I'm sorry. My mistake. I forgot that you insist on fidelity in a relationship. Ashton Walker, you are going to be stuck with me for the rest of your life if we ever do get married."

"God, I hope so." He released a long, slow breath and wiped the unexpected tear from the corner of his eye. "And you are going to be stuck with me, too."

On the car ride back to the condo following dinner, the cell phone in Krissy Oakes' purse began to blare its own obnoxious ringtone, selected by her during a moment of personal immaturity and indiscretion. She retrieved the phone, checking the caller ID to note an incoming call from Hillary Oakes.

"Hey, Hilly," sang Krissy.

"He's dead, Krissy! He's dead! The son of a bitch shot himself!"

No need to even ask who was dead. Ash, driving his new luxury car down Troost Avenue, had heard the loud wails of Hillary Oakes and immediately knew Bernard Oakes had committed suicide.

Maybe his decision had just been made for him. Maybe he now had an affirmative response for Doug Bryant. Maybe Ashton Walker was now the first Head of Legal for the new Bryant Technology 2.0. No need to debate the decision any longer. *Yeah, $255,000 could go far in buying a nice engagement ring.*

Ash immediately changed course and headed for the behemoth home of the late Bernard Oakes and the very much alive, now emotionally charged, Hillary Oakes. Krissy, stunned and on an emotional roller coaster herself, stared at the passing storefronts, homes and pedestrians. But she shed no tears.

"Could anyone have predicted this? Seen it coming?" asked Ash.

"No . . . yeah." She rested her head back against the leather seat. "I'm thinking some kind of scandal was . . . is brewing at PaseoParkTechnology, like embezzlement. But I'm betting Uncle Bernie has been caught with his pants around his ankles again. I'm putting my money on Hillary being cheated on and getting her ducks in a row to financially castrate Bernie. Yeah, that's my call on this. Final answer."

"I don't know," hedged Ash. "That embezzlement theory sounds like the pièce de résistance to me. He definitely fits the motus operandi. That group of honchos we partied with in Chicago seemed quite capable of skimming and filling their own pockets." He put his turn signal into action while simultaneously turning on to a side street, another car fast approaching. The car blew its horn in response to Ash's late warning. He continued, "You tell me. How do you spend a weekend in one of the finest hotels in Chicago, eat decadent meals, go to a Broadway show sitting in the best seats in the house and it doesn't cost you a dime? I'm placing my $10 on embezzlement." The men's room conversation between Bernie and another PaseoParkTechnology player regarding the manipulation of the small timer's stock profile resurfaced in Ash's memory. *Maybe Uncle Bernie was about to get his hand slapped after being caught with it in the cookie jar.*

As they pulled into the long driveway before the Tudor style house, they counted four police cars and a black cargo van, the silver landau bars of a funeral service provider on its sides. A group of about a dozen neighbors stood clumped together on the sidewalk before the house, their eyes riveted on the new arrivals to the Oakes residence. Hillary fled the house when she saw their car's headlights.

"The son of a bitch!" she raged, "He was shagging a lady he met at a board meeting for some homeless program! And she's married, too! What the hell?"

"I'll take that $10 when you have it," Krissy smugly tossed at Ash.

The new widow was marching towards their car. With the engine now disengaged, her ranting was all the more audible. "I went to drop off a donation of some clothing at the shelter, and I see them in his car on the parking lot in broad daylight! She's giving him a blow job! What an ass!" The group of gathered neighbors began to disperse having had all of their questions answered by Hillary's unscripted report, filling in all of the blanks and then some.

"Did you confront him?" Krissy attempted to hug Hillary but was pushed back. She dropped her rejected arms and allowed the tirade to continue.

"Nah. It was pretty much over between us anyway. I just came home and called my brother in Manhattan. I told him to start drawing up the papers, and to make me a well-kept divorcee."

They stepped back as the gurney and the black body bag were rolled out onto the stones of the front porch. Hillary merely shook her head in anger and hurt as the body was rolled by her and on towards the waiting van.

"How did he do it?" asked Krissy. "You said he shot himself?"

"Hand gun in his big dumb mouth. You should see the mess in the study."

"Ah, no thanks." Krissy brought her hand to her mouth to stifle the surge from her dinner wanting to make a second appearance.

A police detective in the telltale dark suit with the pocket protector displaying his badge and identity, stepped out on the porch to join them. "I think

Chapter 21

Changing of the Guard

Bernard Oakes's memorial service was held in a small auditorium on KCU's campus. It was well attended by local politicians, representatives of philanthropic organizations and employees of PaseoParkTechnology, with none of the attendees obviously knowing the true reprobate Bernie really was. They had always seen the gladhanding side of the man, the one who wrote checks for substantial charitable donations and spoke at high school commencements and civic fundraising galas. They'd never met the man who drank heavily, occasionally snorted cocaine, and would bed almost anyone or anything of the female gender.

The limo provided by the mortuary service picked up Hillary, Krissy, and Ashton at the Tudor house on Sunset Drive in the ritzy section of town. Also sharing the limo was Madilyn Oakes Reinhold, the mother of Krissy Oakes, and former sister-in-law of the deceased. She had driven in from her home in rural Missouri, still looking every bit the member of suburban high society. She was wearing a black dress and tasteful pumps. A vivid scarf in shades of red, purple with a random streak of canary yellow was flounced around her neck. Perhaps the burst of color was her attempt to dis Bernard Oakes one last time with her blatant disregard for the funeral dress code that mandated only somber colors.

"Mom, I'd like you to meet Ashton Walker. He's the one I've been telling you about."

It was Krissy's turn to show off her prize. Face it, Ashton Walker was aging well. His auburn hair was only slightly gray at his temples. The few creases in his forehead and the corners of his hazel eyes served as patina, making him appear somewhat rugged, undeniably viral. He, too, qualified for inclusion in the category of *eye candy*.

"Ashton. I love the name." The woman grasped his hand, taking a small step back to fully appreciate his outward appearance.

"I was named after some guy on a soap opera." *There was that trailer park qualifier again.* "It's very nice to meet you. I'm a big fan of your daughter."

"Well, you are all she talks about when she calls me, so I guess it's mutual."

Ash's own speculation about Madilyn Oakes Reinhold's physical appearance was confirmed to his liking. Her daughter had inherited the woman's finest chromosomes. Madilyn was stunning, giving Ash hope if he and Krissy should ever marry, he would still have glitter and tinsel on his arm until the day his own casket was closed. He found Krissy and her mother were very much alike in facial expressions, even having the same uninhibited laugh that he found arousing at times. Just not today as they all rode together in the family limo to the memorial service for Bernard Oakes.

The four family members sat in a cluster in the first row of the auditorium. Sounding like the opening of line of a joke, a priest, a minister and a rabbi gave eulogies in an attempt to prevent the soul of Bernard Oakes from entering the gates of Hell. Ashton Walker speculated it was too late. Bernie was probably already surrounded by friends and fellow lushes as well as a harem of harlots dancing amongst the flames. He mostly likely had reconnected and now resided alongside those whom he had found comfort with here on earth, continuing on with his overindulgence in immoral deeds now that he held carte blanche to do so.

Following the service, the limo service drove the foursome to the waiting luncheon in one of the ballrooms of a prominent hotel in downtown Kansas City, arranged and paid for by the Board of Trustees for PaseoParkTechnology. Ash excused himself from the family to mingle amongst those from PaseoParkTechnology, them socially kibitzing on company time. He stood amongst the echelon of the eighth floor, congregated around a single table in an attempt to prevent penetration by the peons of the lower floors. But Ashton was given special dispensation. He could shake their hands, talk with them, was almost one of them. Bernard Oakes had made his acceptance possible. *No thanks, Uncle Bernie. I prefer to spend my eternity in heaven among the saints and far removed from the sinners of PaseoParkTechnology.*

Ash was met with condolences and compliments regarding the contributions made by the late Bernard Oakes. The eighth-floor executives who were present confirmed their continued embracing of the senior legal into their social circle. Ash was pelted with, "Don't be a stranger just because Bernie's gone." "Let's have lunch next week." "See you at happy hour at the Chophouse." He was even told, "You and Krissy are still included on the Grand Cayman trip, you know."

He wondered if the invitations to lunch with the eighth-floor execs would cease in a few weeks with Bernie's death being a thing of the past. What about the buddy-buddy greetings in the lobby or on the elevator? Would the executives return to being indifferent to him or to just plain ignoring the peon once again as he walked to his car at the end of his day? Matt Blaylock was probably rubbing his hands together in delight and scheming as to how he could step in as the replacement for Ash in the clique of PaseoParkTechnology honchos.

Wait! Why should he even care any longer? His allegiance to PaseoParkTechnology was no more. He truly was no longer "one of them."

Following the luncheon of roast beef, garlic mashed potatoes, green beans almondine and Bernie's favorite crème brûlée, the foursome returned in the limo to the Tudor house on Sunset Drive. During the shared ride, with the ashes of the deceased now residing in a marble crypt, the living trust agreement came up in their discussion.

"Bernie's last act was probably reviewing the living trust," Hillary shared as the limo took a bounce over a pothole.

"How do you know that?" asked Ash.

"The key to the wall safe was on his desk." The newly crowned widow looked in the reflective finish of the limo's window to search for food particles between her perfectly aligned teeth. "I had to use a Kleenex to touch the lock since a chunk of his brain was stuck to the metal." Hilly seemed to enjoy sharing the unnerving tidbit. "Anyway, I must have spent an hour trying to make sense of the *therefores* and the *wherefores* and the other legal mumbo jumbo. Why can't you lawyers just speak English?"

"So what *could* you decipher from the text?" Ash thought *mumbo jumbo* was an accurate term for basic legalese.

"Well, Krissy, the house is yours. I did get the three George Caleb Bingham's and the title to my hybrid. Woo hoo." A rotating index finger was included for emphasis. "A boatload of charities will receive his money and investments. I guess it's his way of buying forgiveness for all of his transgressions."

"Can you afford the house?" Ash looked to Krissy.

He could only imagine the utility bills, the taxes, the insurance and upkeep for the structure. *Do you quit a steady job when you've just been handed an annual* *real estate tax assessment of $11,000+ a year? Wait, not my problem. We're not married. Not my house...yet.*

"Well . . . I'll have to see. I guess I need to get a lawyer, don't I?" She stuck her tongue out at the lawyer seated next to her in the limo.

In the late evening, Krissy and her mother drank martinis as Ash sipped his gin and tonic in the lobby of Madilyn's hotel. Ash heard stories, both happy and depressing, regarding Krissy's childhood, culminating with the death of Alan Oakes just off the coast of Virginia. Krissy excused herself to the ladies' room leaving Ash alone with the remarried widow. Odd. Nothing was mentioned about Mr. Reinhold, the replacement spouse. Obviously the floundering insurance salesman felt no need to attend the sendoff for Bernard Oakes.

"I . . . I need to talk to you while Krissy is away." Ash swallowed hard. "I'd ask her father, but since that's not possible I'm going to ask you . . . I would like your permission to take Kristen's hand in marriage."

"Well! Aren't you the old fashioned one!" She polished the martini off and signaled the cocktail waitress for another. "Don't insult my daughter," she cautioned. "She makes her own decisions, calls her own shots."

"You don't think I know that? I was just wanting to play nice with you." Ash could feel his cheeks taking on a little warmth resulting from Madilyn's blunt response. He guessed he now knew where Krissy got her sass and independence.

The slightly impaired woman leaned into Ash. "She's mad about you. You're all I hear about when she calls me. You . . . you keep her feet on the ground. You make her genuinely happy and not grasping at straws like her old lady." Maybe he now knew where the replacement husband stood with Marilyn Oakes Reinhold. "Sure. Go ahead. Pop the question and be sure to send me an invitation."

"We will. After all, you'll be the mother of the bride."

She raised the fresh martini in a toast. "To happiness without a price tag but coming straight from the heart." She took a sip, ending with a slight slurp. "Ta da," sang the woman.

It was the same culminating response usually given by Krissy when there was no surprise ending, everything just going along as expected, going just as planned… or totally out of one's control.

Chapter 22

Another Upheaval

Ash waited the full week following Bernard Oakes's memorial service. A week for the dust to settle and the two cardboard boxes that now contained Bernie's legacy to be removed from the CFO's vacant office. Those boxes were deposited on Ash's desk to be dealt with as he saw fit. He considered putting the boxes into the dumpster by PaseoParkTechnology's loading dock on his way to his car that evening. But instead, he chose to put them on the floor of the closet in the condo's second bedroom. Perhaps with time, Krissy would have a softened opinion of her uncle and would want to see what was thought to be important enough to be kept by those who supposedly knew him well as they packed up his office.

The covey of executives on the eighth floor continued to acknowledge the sixth-floor peon, an exec even stopping by Ash's office one afternoon to inquire as to how the family was doing. Ash wondered if the man just wanted Hilly Oakes' phone number now that the perky princess was widowed and available again. He wondered if maybe the exec was just looking for a roommate on the upcoming Grand Cayman trip.

The following Monday, Ash took his typed letter of resignation into the office of PaseoParkTechnology's Head of Legal, Louis Finley. He cleared his throat as he stood before the massive desk.

"Have you got a minute, sir?" Ash tapped the folded letter in his open palm.

"Stop with the sirs. We all play for the same team here." The usually peevish man pushed his coffee cup to the side while simultaneously opening his center desk drawer and sweeping the travel brochure into it. He gestured towards one of the empty chairs before him.

"Well... not for much longer." Ash remained standing. Leaning across the substantial desk, he passed off the folded page to the man in his starched white shirt. "I'm leaving PaseoParkTechnology."

The man's face took on a truly baffled visage. "Why would you want to do that? Just because Bernie's gone doesn't mean—" He opened the document and began scanning the script.

"No, I had another job offer the morning Bernie died. This was already in the works."

"Can . . . can I ask with whom?"

"Bryant Technology 2.0."

The gentleman's eye ricocheted around his office. "Sounds familiar . . ."

"PaseoParkTechnology bought out the initial company about seven months ago. I handled the takeover in Seattle. This is a spinoff started by one of the sons." Ash started to sit but thought better when he saw the Head of Legal's jaw beginning to constrict and the jugular vein in his neck giving off a couple of distinct pulsations.

"Hmm." He issued a fatherly growl. "Doesn't sound like too solid of a move on your part. Are you sure you want to do this?"

"I've never been more certain of anything in my life," Ash lied.

"Well, if there's an opening you can always come back here you know," he said as nothing more than empty words. He tossed the letter where the travel brochure had been on his desktop. The man looked around his office, searching for words that might change the young lawyer's mind.

Ash felt his brain going into overdrive and the brake on his own jaw releasing, "No, I won't be coming back here. I want to work for a company with scruples and high standards." A deafening silence followed the squealing burnout of Ash's proclamation.

The Head of Legal's eyes narrowed. His voice could only be described as that of a rabid dog's low growl, seconds before its attack. "Take your pathetic self out of this office! You're an ungrateful toady! Oakes had you pegged. You think you'll be appreciated by this, this start up? You think you'll get as far there without Bernie Oakes pulling strings for you?" The letter of resignation was suddenly shredded into multiple pieces. Ash stared at what remained of that which had taken him at least an hour to compose, now strewn across the executive's desktop.

administrative assistant who had brought him the boxes. He always thought she had a crush on him, her staring at him as he stood at the copier and often offering to do the menial task for him.

Ash saw Matt Blaylock leaning against the open doorframe of the office that he still retained. Matt shared loud enough for all present to hear, "Well, I guess it really isn't who you know or even who you blow. I guess one needs to just be a team player."

"See you in court, Blaylock." Ash's remark was met with a confused look from the other attorney. "I'm the new Head of Legal at Bryant Technology 2.0."

"Never heard of them," Matt concluded with a dismissive humph.

"You will. You most certainly will."

Ash drove home, the two boxes in the backseat. He unloaded his car into the waiting elevator. Once on the third floor of the condo building, he carried one box on his hip and used the toe of his shoe to push the other box down the worn-out carpet of the third-floor hallway. The cardboard carton would occasionally hit areas where the nap was reduced to the jute backing of the carpet, causing Ash to almost tumble over the stalled box. Hearing the woosh, woosh, woosh just outside the door to 3C, Krissy opened the unit's front door to see what was making the odd sound.

"Hello, Krissy Oakes. Meet the *fired* Ashton Walker."

"You're kidding, *right*?"

"Oh no. No. I was told to get the fuck out, complete with an escort from PaseoParkTechnology Security."

"Oh Ash . . ." She stood back to let him bring the two boxes into the condo. "At least you already have another job. Make yourself a drink and I'll hurry up dinner."

Ash flopped on the living room sofa, kicking off his loafers and bringing his sock feet to rest on the edge of the distressed coffee table. He took a significant swig from his gin and tonic. He pondered if what had just happened to him had really happened. Fired? Fired? This was a first. Would it be a last? Would he be fired in the future from Bryant Technology 2.0? Wasn't being fired supposed to be a bad thing? Then why did he feel so damned relieved?

"I'm thinking a visit from that Gestapo guard, or maybe that school teacher would be good tonight," Ash called to Krissy, puttering in the dinky kitchen. "Handcuffs, whips, maybe even those clampy things again…"

Sticking her head from the kitchen doorway, "I'm sure it can be arranged."

"We're definitely not playing doctor tonight. Oh no, no." He dramatically gave a decisive head shake, "I already had a visit with a proctologist today." His hips immediately hovered above the sofa, his eyes opened to their maximum roundness. "Lou already gave me that exam today."

Krissy released a shrieking laugh. "Oh, baby!" She continued the banging of pots and pans in the kitchen as she prepped their dinner. "Well, I talked to Hilly today and now that she's a *widow*," Ash could almost hear the eye roll in the living room, "she's going to move back to New York. She's going later this week to look for an apartment, and she said we should stay in the house and start deciding what to keep and what to pitch."

"Yeah, that sounds like a plan." He brought the back of his head to rest on the crest of the sofa, releasing a groan audible only to himself.

It was a *plan* that Ash wanted no part of. Ash truly had no interest in the house. If a bolt of lightning were to strike it tonight, burning the place to the ground, at least they could collect the insurance. He liked his condo. He could easily afford his condo. He wanted to grow old in his condo, like his neighbors. He wanted to die in his condo as a couple of his neighbors already had done. No hoopla, no fanfare.

He looked at Krissy in the kitchen, as she gyrated her shapely hips to a song from the 50s playing on the surround sound. What was it with women with money, who came from money? They always had that same aura. The house of the late Bernard Oakes was built for the likes of her, designed for her type. It was spacious and well suited for parties and holiday celebrations. It had custom designed closets built for trendy wardrobes and massive collections of expensive shoes. The house had her name all over it. But it wasn't for him.

The ever-practical lawyer could only view the house as being expensive: taxes, heating, cooling, maintenance. Even if he made $255,000 a year and she continued her not-for-profit, replacing Hilly's vacant position, Ash didn't think they could even afford the three-car garage of the house. They'd need a weekly yard service. Corrine would need an entire day to just clean the first floor. What about the second floor?

As they ate dinner Krissy suggested inviting Meredith and her two kids to the Tudor house one evening for dinner. The kids could swim in the heated built-in pool in the back yard.

A swimming pool… Great. Something else out of his budget range.

***

"This place is amazing," gushed Meredith, flanked by her two children as they stood in the entry foyer of the late Bernard Oakes's earthly home. The threesome looked like tourists on a double decker bus tour of New York City, gawking in all directions.

"Yeah, if you make a boatload of money." Ash stood by his younger sister, visually taking in the house along with her. The dark millwork and ornate wall sconces were abundant. The costly furnishings, too sizeable for most suburban

"Yeah." Ash took a deep breath. He looked at Meredith with a smile indicative of his inner joy. "When her mom was here for the funeral, I asked for her permission to marry Krissy."

"Oh, Ash!" gushed Meredith. "What did she say?"

"She told me Krissy makes her own decisions and calls her own shots. She told me to not be bothering her with some old-fashioned, traditional nonsense."

"Sounds like she knows her daughter well. She sounds like she taught her daughter well." Meredith called to her kids, "Another fifteen minutes and then we have to go home."

She was met with the expected, "But mom! We're having fun!"

"I figure I'll give Krissy another few weeks to get her life back together, and then I'll do one of those ooey-gooey, over-the-top proposals you see on YouTube. I'm going to a jeweler next week to pick out a ring."

"This will be a great house to raise kids in." Meredith felt a twinge of jealousy at the thought of a mother and *a father*, and their kids living a life of such comfort and opulence.

"Let's not rush things." His wary eye roll was a given. "I don't want my life consumed trying to manage and maintain this place."

Once Meredith and the kids left for their modest home in Overland Park, Ash and Krissy shared a lounge chair by the pool. The lights shining from beneath the pool's water produced a romantic glow illuminating the well-established trees of the backyard. The sounds of crickets and tree frogs served as romantic violins in the background. The evening temperature was perfect for snuggling and soft kisses.

"Life is good," Krissy cooed.

"It can be." Ash hedged, still not comfortable with all of the sudden changes in his own status quo.

"Admit it. You're going to miss the people in the condo building. You're even going to miss Doris."

He dramatically tossed his head back into the plastic webbing of the chair. "Never!" He then took a careful look at Krissy's face. "Are you doing okay? Are you holding up okay with all the stuff that's gone down in the past couple of weeks?"

"Yeah . . . maybe I'm a little tired. But yeah, I'm good."

"Meredith just asked. She's noticed a change in you. She said you haven't been as chatty as usual. I've still got a week before I start at Bryant Tech. Let me know if I can do anything to help you."

"Yeah . . . can you massage my feet?"

"Your wish is my command." He moved to sit on the end of the lounge chair, taking a narrow foot into his two hands and he gently began working over her tight tendons.

Ash and Krissy spent their first night in the stately house on Sunset Drive. She found the thought of sleeping in the same bed Bernie and Hilly had shared a bit macabre, perhaps more so disgusting. Krissy opted to sleep in the queen size bed in her old room. Ash just shook his head at the mauve and pistachio spray paint finish of her canopy bed and furniture, the handy work of a twelve-year-old Kristin Louise Oakes.

Ash fell asleep almost immediately. He was finding so many changes in his life and his routine taking its toll on him. His appetite had dwindled, and his body tension wasn't responding to his attempts to jog or exercise. Most nights he tossed and turned for almost an hour before finally falling asleep. But not tonight. Even with him being in a strange house, in a strange bed he was asleep within a few minutes. He'd occasionally stir with an unexpected sound but would doze right back off to dreamland. That was until 2:12 a.m.

"Ash! Wake up! Get up!"

"Wha-?"

"Get up, get dressed. We're going home."

"What? It's, it's two o'clock in the morning," he said, locating the small clock on the nightstand. "What do you mean we're going home? Krissy, we *are* home." He sat up to see Krissy fully dressed, standing at the foot of the bed.

"This place is giving me the creeps. I keep hearing the floors creak and things popping. It's Uncle Bernie! He really doesn't want us here!" She wrapped her arms around herself, giving a tight hug.

"Krissy! Will you listen to yourself? If you don't chill, the only place I'm taking you is to a psychiatric unit."

"Well, at least I'll be out of here! Ash, take me home! Now!"

Ashton Walker, awake from Krissy's hostile takeover of his sleep stretched, yawned and brought his feet to the cold floor of the bedroom. He credits the shock of the chilled surface in granting him an exquisite revelation! He could get his own way if he just accommodated the woman, if he just played along with her nonsense. He joined her in her nightmare, snatching his own clothing from the nearby chair.

"Yeah. I was having a tough time sleeping too. You're right, I kept hearing things, too. Yeah, creaking and, and a couple of like low moans. Maybe the windows don't seal well . . . Wow, new windows will be expensive for this place." *Was his last statement a little too much, maybe a little overkill?*

Krissy was already dressed, setting a new record time. Ash didn't even fully button his shirt but merely pulled his sweater over the gapping fabric. They made certain the front door was locked, and they jumped into his crossover, heading back to downtown Kansas City and the twelve units of Parc LeMay.

"I want to sell the house." Krissy said, adjusting the vent on her side of the dashboard as they drove along the vacant streets.

"Are you sure about that?" Ash feared looking overanxious by immediately jumping on the bandwagon. "You might want to—"

"Absolutely. I can't live in that house."

"Well, sleep on it, well what's left of tonight, and we can call a realtor in the morning."

Ash wondered how soon the Wilber Realty office opened in the morning? He had spied a sign for one of their sales agents in another yard on Sunset Drive. He hoped the agent farmed the neighborhood and already had a potential buyer for the Tudor home with its five bedrooms, seven bathrooms, and ghost of Uncle Bernie.

Chapter 23

Cathartic Disclosures

"Do we have to report to the purchaser the fact Uncle Bernie blew his brains out in the study?" Krissy questioned as the car slowly rolled through the flashing red light of an intersection, no other vehicles in sight. The dashboard clock confirmed it was now 2:58 a.m.

"I'm thinking there may be something about the disclosure of someone expiring in a residence. I'd have to look up the local statute." Ash pushed down on the accelerator. "Right now, I just want to get back to bed." The silence of the night resumed save for the hum of the car's V-6.

"Does a lowlife asshole count?" she angerly raged, her shrill voice catapulting Ash awake from his pre-dawn stupor.

"What?" Ash's head snapped to look at the location of the emotional outburst. "Whoa! Talk about speaking ill of the dead!"

"My mother always told me not to speak ill of the dead, but she never said I couldn't sing and dance." Krissy raised her clenched fists into the air and did a wiggle from her waist up.

Ash wondered if he was watching a cathartic episode unfolding in the front seat of his car. He didn't have to wait long to find out.

"Bernie never touched me. He never hurt me directly, but it was what I had to witness . . . How could some women have so little self-respect?" She forced her fingertips into the roots of her hair.

Krissy talked about the naked woman who overdosed in the bathtub of the master bathroom, a fourteen-year-old Krissy watching the paramedic inject the Narcan to revive her. She told about the time when she was fifteen years old, going into the kitchen for a glass of water during the night and seeing a woman lying naked on the kitchen work island while Bernie slammed his goods into her. She recounted the time she came home early from a high school dance with her date and observing a woman crawling through the living room in only a dog collar attached to a leash.

She had obviously witnessed a pro at depravity and sexual stimulation. What lessons had she learned from her observations? What skills did she add to her repertoire? Ash wondered if her antics in the motel room of the Prince Edward Motel resulted from watching the master at work, Bernie orchestrating fantasies with his many partners. Ash pondered if Krissy found it as tantalizing as he did, him in handcuffs, her calling the shots in the Camdenton motel. Or was she dutifully carrying out what she thought a man expected, even demanded. Had the pleasure truly been all his?

The purging of her memory in the early morning hours depleted her remaining strength and energy. By the time they pulled into the garage of the condo building, Krissy was sound asleep. Ash lifted her limp form from the front passenger seat and struggled to carry her dead weight to the garage elevator. He hoped he wouldn't lose his grip as they rode the elevator to the third floor and traversed the length of the hallway to their front door. She stood only long enough for him to get his door key from his pants pocket, then he dropped her to the sofa where she merely twisted on to her side, her shapely body rounding into a fetal ball. After covering her with a blanket, Ash collapsed onto his own bed, falling fast asleep. He was home.

On Sunday afternoon, the overanxious realtor from Wilber Realty came to Unit 3C of Parc LeMay. Her face relaxed when it was clarified that the property to be sold was *not* the condo unit, but the stately house on Sunset Drive. She couldn't mask the fact she was looking forward to a substantial commission based on the projected sale price of $1,495,000 for the luxurious house in its high-end location. No, the condo was not for sale. It was home.

Fearing a possible change of heart on Krissy's part, Ash s breathed a sigh of relief when Krissy told the realtor that all dealings were to go through her attorney, Ashton Walker. Krissy was done with anything that would remind her of the perverted Bernard Oakes. She never wanted to hear the man's name ever again. She, too, was home.

***

Thursday afternoon, Ash met the same realtor at the uninhabited house for an initial walk-through, noting changes to be made to get the house ready for the market. This time the agent's face betrayed her pleasure with the numerous upgrades and amenities that made the house standout above other such houses in the neighborhood. She predicted the sale to be fast, even entertaining the possibility the house could bring on a bidding war with a cash offer. The current market, with the increased demand for homes in the Kansas City area, was bringing on just such a spike in offers and contracts. Ash gave a quick silent prayer, *From your lips to God's ears.*

On the way home, Ash stopped by a small jewelry store with the intent of selecting an engagement ring. The jeweler suggested a small, temporary ring, showing Ash a velvet lined tray of simple bands with simple stones. He suggested Ash give Krissy a pseudo-engagement ring with his proposal and allow her to choose her own ring with her acceptance of his marital overture. The man sounded weary of having rings returned, but happy to sell a much pricier bobble as a replacement. The jeweler placed the ring in a small red velveteen box for the presentation, and Ash left with the simple gold band with a cubic zirconia solitaire shining in the center just for this purpose.

Ash put the small box into his pants pocket and carried the folder of paperwork from the real estate agent in such a way as to conceal the small protrusion on his hip. He entered the condo to see the backside of Krissy assembling dinner in the galley-like kitchen. He saw the dining room table was already set, noticing too the surrounding ambiance was a little nicer than usual. Music softly played over the surround sound, and candles were lit on the table. Maybe life was finally returning to normal.

"Dinner will be ready in about ten minutes. How did it go with the real estate agent?" she called to him.

"Good. There's only a few things that don't meet code. I'm going to go wash up." He slipped down the hallway, thinking he probably looked even more suspect by walking on his toes.

As scheduled, Krissy put the pork loin, the steamed brussels sprouts, and the sautéed carrots on the waiting trivets centered on the dining room table. She sat herself down at her usual place just as Ash returned to the open living/dining area. He was about to take his chair when Krissy stopped him.

"Ash, I forgot something in the oven. Will you get it for me?"

"Sure."

He entered the kitchen, going to the drawer next to the stove and retrieving a couple of crocheted pot holders. He opened the oven door, bending forward in expectation of a baking sheet or a ceramic crock. But neither item was in the illuminated oven. It was then Ash noted the missing rush of hot air into the room. The oven wasn't even turned on, the pork loin having been prepared in a slow cooker on the kitchen's counter. And he saw only one solitary item on the middle shelf of the oven. He turned towards Krissy, still seated in her chair at the dining room table, her looking intently back at Ashton Walker.

Ash took one of the crocheted potholders, reached into the oven and removed the single item. He looked at Krissy, thrusting the item towards her and he succinctly stated, "There's only a roll in the oven."

"No, Ashton Walker, there is a bun in the oven."

"That's what I said. Bun. Roll. And there's only one of them."

"Yes . . . there's *a bun* . . . in *the oven*."

The confusion on his face was almost comical. "So is *the bun* for you or for me?"

Her frustration was becoming evident. "I believe *the bun* is for *us*, Ashton Walker," she huffed.

Ash leaned against the doorway of the kitchen. His brain was desperately trying to break the code of her encrypted message. *"Bun? Oven?"* He began to stand erect, bringing himself to his full height of 6'1".

"I thought you said you had one of those, those AEDs implanted in your wrist?"

"I believe it's an IUD . . . although you look like you could use a defibrillator yourself right about now."

"You're . . . you're pregnant?"

"Ah, yeah . . . I'm thinking maybe about six weeks. My doctor won't see me until 8 weeks, but the pee-on-a-stick test says I'm pregnant." She lifted the plastic stick hidden in her lap, flashing its double lines at Ash. "Ta da."

Her "ta da" didn't have its usual verve and vitality. It even lacked its consistent sarcasm. This "ta da" revealed Krissy's fear and apprehension. It told Ash that all was not right in Unit 3C, at least in the mind of Kristin Louise Oakes.

Ash slid one of the dining room chairs next to Krissy's chair and collapsed his lean frame onto it. He took his palm and placed it against her abdomen. Feeling nothing at this early stage of the game, he looked into her eyes trying to find the answers to the many questions swirling like a tornado in his head. He could feel his own throat drying, his pulse picking up and a lightheadedness overtaking him as the reality of the situation began to set in.

"Are you okay with this?" she tentatively asked

"It doesn't really matter to me." The usually articulate lawyer had bumbled his response. He pressed his lips together in an attempt to preempt another faux pas from escaping. "Well, yes it does, but I mean... I'm not the one that's pregnant." With a deep breath, "So, how do you feel about, about this?"

"I, I've thought it through. I'm not real happy with the timing. The business is going through an upheaval with Hilly leaving. You're changing jobs into a relatively unknown venture." She placed her hand over his as it remained in place. "I called my mom when I saw the YES sign. Since she's had experience with this type of situation and I was an absolute mess when I saw the two lines... I just needed to talk to her, hear her thoughts."

"And..." *Was he actually hurt that Krissy hadn't told him first?*

"She asked me if we were both so stupid we didn't know where babies came from or how to prevent them. I guess I was just so naïve as to think birth control was 100% foolproof, and now I have irrefutable proof that it's indeed faulty." Krissy paused to take the serving spoon and ladled a serving of carrots onto her plate, then she reached for Ash's plate to do the same. "My mom was younger than me when she had me . . . So, even if you don't want to stick around, I think I can do this by myself. I can survive, even thrive on my own. My mom did it, and I turned out okay . . . I guess."

A sweet smile started forming on his lips. Ash took the platter of pork loin and placed a serving on his plate, then a serving onto Krissy's plate. "Kristen Oakes, you're not doing anything by yourself . . . We're, we're in this together."

Her brave façade began to crumble. Krissy's lower lip quivered, her chin dimpled, and the tears came forth. Ash met her in a hug that served to comfort both of them. He managed to hear her muffled "I had a feeling that you'd say something like that" from beneath his coddling arms.

"Here! Wait here!" He jumped up from his dining room chair, catching the chair before it could hit the hardwood floor.

Ash darted from the dining room and down the hallway to the second bedroom, the home office. He retrieved the pseudo-engagement ring from the bottom desk drawer where he had just hidden it. He retraced his steps back to the dining room with the ring box tucked in his hand. He paused briefly to compose himself, allowing his heartbeat to slow just slightly before reentering the open room.

"Well, this isn't exactly the way I had planned to do this." He dropped to his knee next to her chair. "Kristen Oakes, will you marry me?" He produced the small red box, opening it to expose the stand-in ring. Taking her hand, he slipped the dainty gold ban with its fake diamond over her ring finger. She brought her hand upward to study the new addition to her left hand. He quickly clarified, "It's just a substitute for this occasion! You can pick out a ring more to your taste when I return this one to the jewelry store."

She twisted her hand backwards, then forward, viewing the polished gold from different angles, the light from the chandelier reflecting with each turn. "I . . . I don't know. I kind of like this one. It's . . . simple." She paused to hold her hand next to the flicker of the burning candle on the dining room table. "I think I'd like a simple ring to remind me to keep life simple and uncomplicated, and to just enjoy the ride."

Ash rose from his knee to seat himself next to the woman he loved. He took her decorated hand into his, looking at the new enhancement. "I like that...keeping it simple. But I'm thinking you'd probably prefer a ring with a real diamond and not just a wannabe diamond."

Krissy scrunched her face into a confused frown. "Are you sure you're not asking me to marry you just so you can get the money from Uncle Bernie's estate? The sale of the house? My trust fund?"

"Hey." He made his best insulted face, his mouth rounding like that of a fish. "Monday morning I'll be the Head of Legal for a tech company that is going to one day make PaseoParkTechnology look like a preschool. I don't need your stinkin' money."

"Go get 'em, Mr. Ambulance Chaser."

Ash had a sudden epiphany. "We're going to have to sell the condo!" he blurted.

"What? Why?"

"This place isn't conducive to kids. The schools aren't bad, but they aren't the best in this area. There's no playground or backyard for a swing set."

"Slow down! Can we get through a wedding first? How about labor and delivery? The kid is going to live in a playpen for a couple of years. We've got time. Kids grow up in apartments in downtown Manhattan all the time, and they survive."

"True . . . So, who knows besides your mom?"

"Just my mom. I didn't know myself until this morning. I just figured I had terminal cancer and that's why I was feeling like I was about to die at any moment." Krissy rose from her chair to straddle Ash's legs. There was her signature head tilt, the same seductive smile she had gifted him the morning they met in the Legal Department of PaseoParkTechnology. "How about this, Ashton Walker? After dinner, why don't I get into that platinum wig and rainslicker while I can still fit into it, and we go reduce your stress level?"

"You can . . . we can still have sex?"

"It's not like I can get anymore pregnant than I already am."

PaseoParkTechnology. He sat himself down in the worn wooden desk chair on tarnished brass rollers, giving a rock to test its stability. He looked across the room at the vacant wall of exposed fire brick also showing its advanced years. *Maybe he'd go to one of the Kansas City street fairs and find a few suitable prints to add some warmth and color to his new office.*

With the first box unpacked and the second box awaiting on his desktop, Ash turned the lamp on his desk off and located the open door to the long, narrow conference room that would house his first meeting of BT2.0. As the Head of Legal, he had already decided he wouldn't forbid use of the abbreviation in conversations, only on written correspondence. Doug was already seated at the head of the table, two women and another gentleman were awaiting the start of the meeting with the equally new CEO. Ash took a seat next to the other male, already picking teams.

"Help yourself," invited the CEO, tipping his head towards the spread of bagels and cream cheeses centered on the table. The same bagelry provided paper plates and napkins, their logo prominently displayed on them. A couple of carafes of coffee and a small bowl of creamers and sweeteners sat on a worn cafeteria tray. Ash looked down to see a ceramic coffee mug waiting in front of each participant bearing the newly designed logo for BT2.0.

"I don't mind if I do." He took a small plate, selected a multigrain bagel and smeared it with honey cream cheese. He filled his new coffee cups with decaf, fearing an overdose of caffeine would cause his nervous system to short-circuit with his current level of inner stress. Looking at the branding in its vibrant red, Ash wondered if there would be a day when the simple logo design would be as recognizable as the swoosh of Nike or the hidden arrow in FedEx.

One additional male joined the soiree. Standing in the doorway he weighed his choice of seats, choosing to sit with the women. He flashed a smile across the table at Ash and the other male, then gave a tip of his head towards the women and a hike of his eyebrows, suggesting he had picked the right team to be with. Ash weakly smiled and shook his head at the guy's display of sexism.

"I'd close the door, but we're the only ones here, and there should be no one else in the building to eavesdrop on us. But more importantly we have nothing to hide, nor will this company ever have anything to hide. I'll be addressing the issue of integrity more during this meeting." He took a sip from his own cup of coffee, cleared his throat, and with that Doug Bryant brought the groundbreaking meeting to order.

"Once again, welcome to Bryant Technology 2.0's Big Adventure. I'd like to start this morning with everyone introducing yourself, sharing your background and telling something about who you are as a person. And indulge me, ladies:

everyone tell us your age. I want to make a point at the end of this meeting. We'll begin with Maggie."

"I'm Maggie Malinek, Head of Human Resource. I left this same position with Via Technology, having worked at another tech firm before them . . . no names mentioned. I still have nightmares about their hiring practices. I'm married and my husband is able to work online, so he's joining me in this move. I went to a small state university in western Kentucky. You've probably never heard of it. Go Racers! Oh, I'm thirty-seven."

Ash wondered *what it is about women and their fixation with college team mascots? What's a "racer"? Was it possibly another name for a penis?*

"I'm Laura Dulin. I'm Head of Public Relations and Communications. I took a couple of years off to raise my son, but Doug remembered me from our college days and he thought I'd be a good fit. I was the Head of Events for Needless Markup in Dallas . . ." She scanned the eyes focused on her to see if everyone had made the connection to the high-priced store chain. Maggie mouthed the true moniker to Ash and the man seated to his left. They both acknowledged her clarification, now getting it themselves. "I'm now divorced, a single mom, and I can't wait to throw a good party for Bryant Technology 2.0. I'm thirty-five."

"I always enjoy a good party." The man seated to Laura's left looked like he hadn't been invited to a party since a birthday gathering of his friends in grade school. "I guess I'm the senior citizen by the looks of everyone here. I'm forty-two. I'm head of security: that is firewalls and virus detection. I graduated from Poly, the only Poly that counts, that is. I worked at a government facility. If I tell you where, I'll have to kill you." No one laughed.

"Well, senility has set in. You forgot to tell us your name," Doug Bryant teased.

"Brett Childress. It happens even more so these days. I can forget the simplest things."

"Should we be worried about dementia? Alzheimer's?" Ash joked, followed by a chorus of polite laughter from those in attendance.

Moving across the oblong table, the introductions came to Ash. "I'm Ashton, just Ash, Walker. Doug stole me away from PaseoParkTechnology right here in Kansas City. I graduated from KCU, also here in Kansas City. I guess you can tell I don't get out much. I'm now the Head of Legal. Something personal about me? Well, last night I found out I'm going to be a dad and I proposed to the mother of my baby. I'm happy to report that she said yes." He did a quick scan of faces and found no judgmental reactions, only smiles and mouthed congratulations. "And, I'm going to turn thirty-three this week."

"Wow! It's quite a week for you!" Doug beamed.

Chapter 25

Life on the Spin Cycle

"Ash? Vi Fabick."

"Hey, Vi. HOA problem? Please don't tell me another water pipe broke in the lobby? If it did, I wasn't responsible this time! Honest!" Ash cradled his cell phone beneath his chin. He finished the last line of the paragraph he was typing on his laptop.

"Oh Junior," she laughed. "Well, its potentially just another kind of disaster. The company insuring the building wants to raise our premiums significantly. That'll effect our assessments greatly, and I know the residents won't be happy. I guess since the insurer had to buy us a new lobby, they're going to try to stick it to us now to recoup their losses."

"Really? I'm treasurer and I haven't heard anything to this point. Usually I receive all the communications from the insurance company. They haven't contacted me since letting me know the claim was satisfied on their end."

"Uh...uh, they, they sent me a letter. We, we need to meet tomorrow evening. Just the exec board to discuss this."

Ash sighed. "Tomorrow's my birthday. Krissy wanted to go out to dinner to celebrate."

"Well, can we just meet afterwards? It won't take but a few minutes, hopefully. Just call me when you're on your way back to the building after dinner."

Ash was hoping to enjoy a leisurely birthday dinner and perhaps a little role playing in the master bedroom in lieu of dessert. He'd received a firm *no* from Krissy on reenacting a scene or two from an erotic novel he'd read as an undergrad. *Maybe she'd agree to being the farmer's daughter with him being the city boy, down on the farm for the first time.*

He also knew for a fact the elderly residents of the building tended to fixate on minutia, having nothing important in their lives to serve as a distraction. Some could work themselves up into an absolute frenzy over a burned-out lightbulb in the stairwell or a squeak in a door hinge for the trash chute. It probably was better to just meet and tackle the issue of the increase in premiums head on, preventing a flare up in their anxiety level.

Krissy sat across from Ash in the Ethiopian restaurant he had been wanting to try. The waiter had delivered the H'mbasha with a single birthday candle burning in the flatbread.

"Well, happy birthday, Ashton Walker. I hope it's a good one."

"It's sure going to be an eventful year, that's for sure." He inflated his cheeks and then blew the single candle out.

"One day, one step at a time. So . . . what are you thinking for a wedding? Indoor? Outdoor? Themed?"

"Isn't that your responsibility? Don't you make all of those decisions?"

"Not when it's under these circumstances." She made a two fingered point at her waistline. "Like you said, we are in this together and *immediately*." Krissy resumed picking at the food that remained on her plate, either not hungry or nauseous once again.

"How about the two of us before a judge? After all, we don't have a lot of family, not many friends."

"You make it sound so pathetic." *Was she going to cry?*

"Well, let's sleep on it. We've got at least six months to make a decision, and we can even wait until after the baby comes." *Was he going to cry?*

"No, most definitely *pre*baby. I want our last names to be the same on the birth certificate."

"You're going to change your name?"

"Yes? Is there are problem with that?"

"I just remember Bernie, and even your mom, telling me how independent you are."

"Maybe I just want to distance myself from the Oakes side of the family. I don't have a lot of fond memories, remember?"

"Kristin Walker . . ." He said it aloud. "That works."

"Any ideas yet for the first dance? If we wait too long we might have to dance to the Beer Barrell Polka with me being the barrel!"

"Well, you'll be a beautiful barrel." He envisioned the woman of his dreams being rotund and radiating the glow of motherhood. "A toast!" Ash raised his water glass. "To the most gorgeous barrel on this planet."

"That'll be me!" And after a split-second pause, "Ta da!", the magic having returned to her salute.

Ash wondered if now was the right time, maybe more so pondering if there ever would be a really good time to ask. He decided to jump right in. "On a different topic, did Bernie leave a suicide note? Did he ever give a reason why he'd do such a thing?"

Krissy let her bottom lip jut forward and allowed her vertebrae to compress. "I . . . I don't know. I would think Hilly would have said something if he did. Why do you ask?"

"Because I would think a man of his stature wouldn't just off himself over his infidelity. You said he has a bad track record, right?"

"Yeah. Four marriages and a punch card at the family planning clinic."

"You know this for a fact?"

resemble the puckering of a prune any more if she tried. Ash intercepted her scorn and condemnation when their eyes met, her quickly looking away.

Ash thought back to Doug Bryant's statement on the effects of age at the first meeting of the department heads for Bryant Technology 2.0. *We need to be young and never age ourselves.* The residents of Parc LeMay had aged themselves, clinging to old social norms and expectations, Doris being the most antiquated of all of them.

Ash wondered, at age thirty-three, what did he still cling to? What could he let go of? What wasn't negotiable?

Chapter 26

I'll Take *Reasons for Suicide* for $200, Mayim

The first few weeks at Bryant Technology 2.0 were not without challenges and unexpected events. Having few prior precedence to follow and a need to create policy as the company took flight caused Ash to work some late hours. As he sat in his office one evening, the clock approaching the dinner hour, he heard a soft knock at his door.

"You have to eat, Ashton Walker."

He smelled the fried chicken before he saw the delivery person was Krissy. She had a cardboard box containing dinner for two: fried chicken, corn on the cob, coleslaw, a few homemade biscuits, and two slices of store-bought apple pie. He began to clear his desk as she filled in the empty spaces with a couple of paper plates and napkins.

"There's a soda machine downstairs. I'll get you a soda. What kind do you want?"

"Water is fine. I'm trying to watch my intake these days."

He gave her an empathetic smile. "Yeah, water's good. Me too."

They ate, comparing their days. Ash relayed that he was enjoying the people that surrounded him, finding them to be like minded and highly motivated. Their energy served as a supplement to his own energy when he needed it the most. With a sudden influx of new clients, Ash had been thinking there would be a need in the not-so-distant future for the assistance of a law clerk. Ash told Krissy it was like Doug Bryant had read his mind, telling Ash to put his feelers out for someone that fit the company's squeaky-clean profile.

"How about that guy you were all buddy-buddy with at PaseoParkTechnology? Myron? Milton?" asked Krissy.

"Matt? I'd be insulted if I was at his level and then offered such a lowly position."

"I don't know if he's bright enough to be insulted, he's so arrogant. Just give him a title, like The Grand Poohbah of Legal, and he'll probably be happy."

"He'd also need to clean up his act. He wouldn't be working with me for long if he pulled some of the deals he has with PaseoParkTechnology." Ash picked out a second piece of chicken from the deli box.

"Can a leopard change his spots?" Krissy rose up to pick out another piece of chicken for herself from the same box.

"No, but I believe they can be tamed." He sucked the savory grease from his thumb. "He really does have a good legal mind. He just needs to learn to use it to the benefit of all parties involved."

She started to take a bite but returned the chicken wing to her plate. "I asked Hilly about a suicide note. She said there was none, at least not that she found. She said she never saw one as she packed up the house. She also said she probably wouldn't have bothered reading it anyway since she had caught him in the act. Sorry bustard."

The office became quiet except for the occasional sound of smacking lips or a moan of pure culinary bliss. In the background could be heard the muffled play-by-play of a baseball game playing online in someone's office. The HVAC system kicked on and carried the smell of the picnic dinner throughout the warehouse's second floor. Within a few minutes, they heard a voice call out from down the hallway, "Next time, bring me some of that fried chicken!"

"You've got it, Doug!" Ash called back. He rocked back in his chair listening to the groan of the old, tired center spring, and then he lowered his crossed ankles onto the edge of his desktop. "Have you given anymore thought to wedding plans?"

"Everyday." She started collecting the empty paper products from his desk top, spying a trashcan between his desk and the wall of windows. "I've got some ideas, but I want to run them by you before I book anything. And don't ask me about the music for our first dance! I just get more and more confused. I think I'm up to seventeen possible pieces."

Ash's cell phone began to buzz where it sat on his desktop. He picked up the phone, focusing on the screen.

"What is it with telepathy or the power of suggestion? It's, it's Matt," he sputtered, and then he turned his attention to take the call. "Blaylock? It's been a long time."

"Yeah, yeah. Have you got a minute?"

Ash raised his eyebrows at Krissy. His feet came back down, now firmly planted flat on the floor. "I've got a few minutes. Things are really starting to pop around here at BT2.0. What's up with you and PPT?"

"Somethings going down here... I, I don't know what, but there were two big acquisitions in the works and they've both been put on hold. Lou has been out of the office at least once a day for a couple of hours or more, and the admin says he's being called up to the eighth floor to meet with the big guns." Ash heard the sounds of a television in the background and the clinking of ice cubes in a glass.

"Did they ever fill Bernie Oakes's position? Maybe they're screening potential CFOs?"

"No, it's something more than that. There are rumors buzzing around . . . something about the Feds and an investigation." He heard Matt take a sip, the ice cubes clinking even louder, now closer to his cell phone.

Ash couldn't squelch his inner euphoria, "You forget. I don't work there anymore. I jumped that ship, and it sounds like *your* ship has sprung quite a leak."

"That's it. Enjoy your bonus points for taking cheap shots . . . I guess I deserve the turnabout. They aren't hiring any additional legal counsel where you are, are they?" A deep sigh revealing a level of inner fear unmasked Matt's condition. "I'm . . . I'm kind of financially overextended. I, I need to have a steady income or I'm gonna lose my car."

"Do you want to be a clerk? Be my assistant?"

"Do you want to kiss my . . . Never mind. I may need to put in my application in a couple weeks. Like I said, I've got to have an income of some sort…" In the background, the sounds could be heard of ice ejecting from an ice maker, the glug-glug of a liquid being poured, Matt's slurp as he took a sip of the beverage. Ash speculated it to be a Scotch on the Rocks, Matt's go-to pain killer when dumped by a girl or passed over for a promotion. "I can't imagine a powerhouse like PaseoParkTechnology going down for the count."

"The bigger they are, the harder they fall." Ash couldn't believe the euphoric sensation he was enjoying with every word of their conversation. "Let me know when you need that application. It's nice to work for a firm that isn't full of itself, thinking they rule the world. They actually consult the peons here and listen to their input . . . I probably can put in a good word for you if you promise to clean up your act and behave."

The phone call ended, and the cell phone was returned to Ash's desktop. Ash brought his interwoven fingers behind his head and looked upwards to study the exposed floor joists that composed his office ceiling.

"Could you hear Matt's side of the call?" he asked Krissy.

"A little. So maybe Uncle Bernie bit the bullet just in time."

"Ouch. Poor choice of semantics." Ash gave off a bruised laugh. "And maybe I escaped just in time too."

"They say everything happens for a reason. I wonder what the reasons are at PaseoParkTechnology?" Krissy rose and began to put her arms through the sleeves of her jacket.

"Sounds like a hint of underhanded dealings on the part of the chiefs. Maybe embezzlement *was* the reason Uncle Bernie checked out early. I'll take that $10 back." He reached across his desk, ruffling his fingertips towards Krissy.

"How about this?" She leaned across his desk providing him with a view down her ballooning cleavage. "I give you $5 back since we are both right about Uncle Bernie's motivations."

"Sounds fair. How about this . . . you find that platinum wig and sunglasses, and I'll leave the $5 on the dresser tonight."

"Works for me, Ashton Walker."

With the cardboard box containing the few leftovers from their dinner being transported between her hands, she turned and let the sway of her hips bring the sleeping soldier in his boxers to stand at attention.

Chapter 27

Life, Death, Downfall

Ash and Krissy went to the office of the OB/GYN she had selected to deliver Baby Walker. They filled out the forms and answered all of the doctor's questions. They both felt an internal flutter at the sound of the baby's heartbeat, and each of them clung to a copy of the ultrasound photo provided by the technician. They decided they didn't want to know the gender, leaving it to be a surprise in the delivery room.

Returning home, Ash was about to drive past the circle driveway before Parc LeMay, heading for the residents' garage door on the backside of the structure. Krissy called out, "A firetruck! An ambulance! Police!"

"Now what?" bristled Ash.

Instead of continuing past the building and turning down the street that led to the residents' garages, Ash pulled into the halfmoon driveway. He and Krissy bolted from the car and into the building's lobby. They were met by two firemen and several residents, their conversations silenced with their appearance.

"What's going on?" asked Ash, slightly out of breath.

"They think Harry's had a stroke." replied Ralph McNeil.

"Not Harry." Krissy barely kept her quivering voice contained. Harry had become a favorite of hers. But then again, not any more than any of the other residents, Doris Pitman included.

"When did it happen? Who found him?"

"His son called Vi and asked her to check on him. He said he'd tried to call his dad several times over the course of an hour, and he didn't answer his phone."

"Any idea when it happened?"

"No."

Ash hesitantly continued his line of questions. "Do you know how bad he is?"

"Not yet."

A gurney with Harry Hume strapped to it, oxygen cannulas in his nostrils, was wheeled through the lobby and past the small group of residents. His eyes were closed and his complexion was pale, bordering on white. The firemen of the lobby were joined by two additional firefighters in their blue polo shirts and navy workpants. They assisted the EMTs in loading Harry into the back of the waiting ambulance.

A visibly upset Vi Fabick joined the group, her purse clutched in her hand, as they stood in the respectful silence of the lobby. "I wonder how long he was laying there? He . . . he looks so bad. I'm going with him to the hospital. Can I call you for a ride home, Ash?"

"Sure. Don't worry about the time."

Vi Fabick dashed out the door and took a seat next to the paramedic in the driver's seat of the ambulance. Ash looked at the aged faces still standing alongside of him in the lobby, seeing only silver hair and an abundance of wrinkles. *There but for the grace of God . . .* He wondered which resident of Parc LeMay would be the next.

That evening, Krissy and Ash lay side by side in bed reading. Ash's phone began to buzz. Without looking, he speculated it was Vi, and he sincerely hoped it wasn't. He had brought her back to the condo from the hospital at sunset. During the car ride she explained Harry was unstable and in critical condition. He wasn't expected to bounce back without a lot of time in therapy. The stroke had been brutal on his brain. The reality was his doctors weren't optimistic as they spoke in hushed voices to Vi and Harry's sons, while standing at the foot of Harry's hospital bed.

Ash's fear was confirmed. She was calling to initiate the condo building's telephone chain. The chain usually didn't convey information the other residents wanted to hear.

"Ash, it's Vi."

"I know . . . Harry didn't make it, did he?"

"No." Her voice caught in her throat. She tearfully concluded, "His boys are going to make funeral arrangements in the morning."

"Well, let me know what the arrangements are . . . We're going to miss his humor around here."

"Yeah . . . yeah . . . I remember him telling me once, 'It's not that life is too short, it's because death is so long.'"

"There's a lot of truth to that. Makes you want to go and take that cruise or climb that mountain, doesn't it?" With a baby on the way, Ash wondered when he'd ever take a cruise, much less ever even see a mountain again.

"Do it, Junior. Take that baby and Krissy and conquer those milestones."

"And you do the same, Vi. Get out there and live . . . I'll make a copy of the HOA Guidelines for the new resident of 1C. Like I said, let me know about the funeral arrangements when you hear anything."

Krissy snuggled into Ash, and they shared the silence, each processing the event of Harry Hume's passing and wishing the gentle soul God's speed.

***

Ash was doing laps of the master bedroom, dressing for work. He opened the top drawer of the crimson red toolchest and selected a tie, one that coordinated with his slate gray slacks. He stepped out on to the balcony of the master suite and studied the clear morning sky, spying a distant frontline on the horizon. Experience told him to choose wisely as he opened one of the battered lockers serving as a closet for his shoe collection. He selected a mildly worn pair that were comfortable for walking, yet still dressy enough to wear in the office. Sitting on the edge of the bed, he looked from his shoes and back through the French doors of the balcony, attempting to determine if the frontline was coming or going.

He joined Krissy, already drinking her morning decaf at the dining room table and perusing her planner for the day. The television in the living room was broadcasting the local weather in the background. Ash stopped to watch, trying to decide if he should drive instead this morning due to the possibility of rain in the late afternoon. The weathercast ended, and before Ash could turn towards the dining room the logo for PaseoParkTechnology flashed onto the TV screen.

"In local news, technology conglomerate PaseoParkTechnology, headquartered right here in Kansas City, has been served with multiple federal warrants for . . ." The news reporter sounded almost gleeful sharing the scandalous headline.

Ashton Walker heard nothing more after the scathing headline. He watched the video of the CEO, the CIO, the CMO, and the CTO being led from the building in handcuffs by men in dark suits. He watched footage of file boxes, with lids secured, being carried out the building's glistening front doors, the same doors Ash had entered and exited more times than he could count. The presumed boxes of evidence were being loaded into a short caravan of unmarked vans.

"For the love of God! Krissy! Look at this!"

Krissy moved her bloating body from the dining table to stand with Ash in the living room.

"Ash! That's, that's a couple of guys from the Chicago trip!"

"No surprise here! That one is . . . was the COO." *George Truex, the guy with plans to retire in two years. Cancel that!*

Krissy's face became panic stricken. "Are . . . are they going to come here, looking for you?"

"Why would they come looking for me?"

"Ash, you ate lunch with those guys at least once, maybe twice every week. You went to Friday happy hours at the Chophouse. You said that they took you into their confidence, shared confidential topics about the company." Panic consumed her face. "You spent a weekend in their company in Chicago! How could you not—" She stopped short of assigning guilt to the attorney..

"I never did anything that would merit a federal warrant! I may have been privy to some of their conversations, but my signature isn't on any of their dealings…" Ash fell silent. "I… I may have given some legal advice to one of them… telling them how to redirect funds without ramifications…"

"Who? Who did you give advice to?" Krissy's eyes were wide with fear.

"The former CFO..." His eyes locked on Krissy as he slowly lowered himself into a wingback chair. "Berny asked me once how to move funds... He said it was a hypothetical situation a businessman had floated over drinks in a bar in Martha's Vineyard when he was visiting Hilly's family..." Ash's hazel eyes began filling with tears. "Matt Blaylock told me one of the schemes being investigated by the feds... It fits the scenario Bernie described, and I expertly told him how I'd handle it..."

Krissy held onto the arm of the sofa as she settled into the cushions. "And here I thought your biggest crime was ordering a medium well porterhouse and a malbec at the Chophouse, using the company's credit card."

The thought of his involvement hadn't crossed Ash's mind, but now it consumed his entire brain. Would they come for him? Was there such a thing as guilt by association? Had he unknowingly, unwillingly done something illegal?

Krissy changed the channel on the TV and the story was being aired by another station. "I wonder if Bernie would be among them if he were still alive?" Her eyes were glued to the television's screen, but her trembling hands sought out the box of tissues kept on the rustic service cart. She covered her trembling lips with a wadded tissue.

With the newscaster moving on to the next piece of Kansas City's dirty laundry, Ash grabbed his cell phone from his pants pocket. He brought Matt Blaylock up in his list of contacts and thumbed the call icon. Matt answered on the second ring.

"Yeah Walker, I've been watching the news all morning. It went down late yesterday afternoon. They sent everybody home until further notice . . ." He swallowed his pride and unplugged his ego, "Can I pick up that job application from you today?"

"What happened? Why are the feds involved?" He wanted to hear Matt reiterate the scheme, now believing he had unknowingly orchestrated a crime.

"Government contracts, under the table deals, price gouging. Take your pick. I guess PaseoParkTechnology figured all the cool kids were doing it, why couldn't they?"

Ash took a deep breath, but his mouth decided to once again override his ability to remain angry at someone or his own feelings remaining hurt by anyone. "Stop by my office today. At least a clerk's job will tide you over until you can find a more fitting position. Who knows, it could turn into a full legal position in the next few weeks if Bryant 2.0 can snag some more of PaseoParkTechnology's clientele with this fiasco." Ash shoved the entire situation to the back of his brain, in need of a diversion, searching for something positive and uplifting upon which the urge to turn his office into a confessional of sorts, him bearing his soul and allowing them to pass judgement on his sins of a loose jaw and an imaginative mind guided by legal precedence. But he feared dragging them into the situation, them *aiding and abetting* an inept lawyer who should have known to *cease and desist* when listening to Uncle Bernie's hypothetical situation.

Krissy cradled the inflating balloon beneath her T-shirt. "Well, you better get on it because Dr. Banner thinks it may only be a matter weeks until our *guest* arrives. It would appear I'm a little farther along than we thought."

"I'll take a shelf or two of books each day this week and then I'll have Matt help me with the heavy moving over the weekend."

"And try to be home on time tonight. There's a welcoming reception in the lobby for the people that bought Harry's condo."

"The nerve of them! A young couple moving into the Old Folks Home. What is the world coming to?" Ash mustered up his best insulted chin launch.

"If we click with them, maybe we can have weekly game nights or double date nights."

"It would be nice to branch out and create a circle of friends our own age . . . Then again, you are ten years younger than me."

"Does that bother you?" Krissy put down the laundry she was folding to take a serious interest in his response.

"Only when I think about it. Looking at the people in this building, there's such a gap between sixty-five and seventy-five, and even more at eighty-five." Ash recalled Doug Bryant's adage stating *age is only a number, it doesn't define a person unless they allowed it to.* "I try not to get too hung up on it, but it's still there."

"Well, look at all of the grandparents Gomer will have living in this building."

"Gomer? You're calling the baby Gomer?"

"You've got something better?" She reclaimed the wadded T-shirt and started to neatly fold it.

"Let me work on that." Ash grabbed his satchel and headed for their front door. "Gomer," he muttered under his breath as he reached for the doorknob. He still continued to take a cautionary peek through the door's peep hole, although a white flag had been raised by both teams and a ceasefire was in effect between he and Doris.

That evening Ash joined Krissy at the soiree to welcome Paul and Lauren Schmidt to Parc LeMay. Both of them were young professionals, recently married and looking a little taken back with the antiqued neighbors now surrounding them. Ash introduced himself to Paul, passing off a red plastic cup containing one of his coveted personal beers.

"They're all really great people. Really. Just watch that one over there in the muumuu. She gets on my last nerve. Her sister is a gem, though." Ash gestured with a toss of his head directed towards Doris and Corinne, the two women now sharing Doris's unit.

"I'll take that into consideration." Paul Schmidt gave an ingratiating nod to Doris, with her returning her best stink eye. "So, Vi says you're going to be a dad pretty soon."

"Yeah, and hopefully a husband before the delivery date. We kind of messed up the order of the *horse and the cart*."

"We did too... Unfortunately the baby was stillborn."

"I'm so sorry." That *there but for the grace of God* thing was immediately resurrected within Ash's soul.

"I wasn't sorry at first, probably more so relieved than anything. I just wasn't ready for parenthood. But I'm not . . . not so sure about that anymore."

"Well, things have a way of working out... That probably wasn't a comforting thing for me to say, was it?" Ash bit his lower lip, hoping to prevent another verbal blunder.

Ash's eyes searched for Krissy and found her seated in a chair, kibbitzing with Betty Stubbs. He mouthed an "*Are you doing okay?*" to her. She smiled back, and then followed the smile with an exasperated look of confirmation to the question he asked her almost hourly.

Before he reached up to turn off the reading lamp above the headboard, Ash and Krissy came together for their routine goodnight kiss. Passing the books each had in-progress to the ebony shelf, they compared notes as to what they had learned about their new young neighbors. They paused to reflect on the sorrow the Schmidts had experienced. Ash and Krissy simultaneously stated their synchronized thought. "We need to set that wedding date!" came in unison.

"And…" Ash hedged, "I don't want to have a first dance at the reception. We kind of already did that anyway the first night I brought you here."

"Hmm, I remember… You holding me tight, pulling me closer to you… You had such a boner!" She palmed his jewels beneath the sheet and blanket, rocking upward to see the startled look on Ash's face.

"Hey! Glenn Miller's music always gives me wood." Over the course of their relatively short relationship he had learned how to be her straight man, able to responds with little or no notice to one of her spontaneously unnerving zingers.

"Oh, geez…" And there was her shrill laugh given in homage to his humor. She maneuvered to her side to face him, rolling as best she could in her current condition. "Why no first dance? Present your argument against a first dance, counselor?"

"I called the courthouse yesterday. I know one of the judges from my days at KCU. He remembered me, and he said he'd be honored to do the deed. We just have to get a license."

"What about a photographer, flowers . . . a reception?"

"Let's see . . . the guest list includes your maid of honor, Hillary, my best man, Matt. Then there's your mother and my sister, niece and nephew. Looks like we won't be needing one of those ballrooms in a hotel. Maybe we can use the waiting room at Union Station and then jump on a train for a honeymoon."

"Ash . . . I want to look back with good memories of our wedding."

"I know." He mustered a placating smile that failed. "Let's talk about this more tomorrow over dinner... Wan Fu Garden?"

"Yeah, we can have our reception at Wan Fu Garden. That'll be memorable!" she huffed.

"No!" Ash burst out laughing. "Dinner there tomorrow night! We can talk about plans over your egg foo yong! Man, you're a little testy these days!"

"I'm sorry. I blame my hormones. I'm not enjoying this ride all that much." She clutched her baby bump as she gave Ash a sweet kiss on the cheek in apology.

The topic was once again moved to the end of the to-do list.

Chapter 29

Spelled Out Clear as Day

Matt and Ash were working as a team, making quick work of disassembling the oak desk in the guest bedroom of the condo. They took the shelves out and the sides apart of the three chintzy book cases, wondering if they could be reassembled and still be sturdy enough to support the weight of legal guides. All the disassembled boards were loaded into the back of the pickup truck Matt had borrowed from his brother-in-law and driven the five blocks to BT2.0. Once at the Power and Light District warehouse an assembly line was formed with Doug Bryant and Joe Stripling, both men working in the office on a Saturday. The foursome brought the pieces into the building and skillfully reassembled them into office furniture in the space assigned to Matt. Before leaving, Ash shook Matt's hand as they stood before the milk glass of his office door. *Matthew Blaylock, Senior Attorney*, glistened in gilded letters on the white glass.

Ash returned to the condo to find a note from Krissy saying she was out shopping for the baby with her mother. He walked down the hallway to reassess the now empty guest bedroom. He took a stress reducing breath, seeing the walls required painting to cover the shadows of where the bookcases had once stood and the carpet was desperate for a deep cleaning. The weight of the oak desk had embedded the circular footpads into the once champagne beige carpet as a permanent reminder of what the room's former purpose was. They would also serve as a reminder of his prior life, a life when all Ashton Walker had was his career and not much more. He was looking forward to his new life as a husband and a father, warding off the sadness his sister predicted if he never experienced either title.

He slid open one of the six-panel closet doors. He saw the few shoeboxes he had placed on the metal rack above him, along with a couple of storage tubs containing what? ... He couldn't recall. Out of sight, out of mind. Eight years in the condo, and he was surprised to find he hadn't accumulated all that much. But, that was all starting to change with the addition of a future wife and soon a baby. His basement storage space was now filled with items Krissy had removed from the Tudor house on Sunset Drive, deciding to keep some things as reminders of her past if and when she chose to relive it. He pondered if there was a need for him to rent one of those storage units near the city limit. And then Ash looked down at the two cardboard boxes resting on the floor of the closet.

They were boxes with the manufacturer's logo on their lids, once containing reams of paper for an office copier at PaseoParkTechnology. The two boxes had been delivered to Ashton Walker when he was still a senior litigator for the now disgraced firm, the company barely a player any longer in the tech industry. The boxes had been brought to him the week following the suicide of Bernard Oakes, containing the contents of the CFO's former office. Ash had never opened the boxes. He had never been the least bit curious as to what the likes of Bernard Oakes would find of importance, what those who had filled the boxes found worth keeping. That was until now.

Ash flopped onto the dingy beige carpet, crossing his ankles. "Criss cross, applesauce." He had heard his sister give the seating directive to her kids dozens of times. He could hear himself giving the same instructions to *Gomer* in a couple of years. He felt his focus giving way to memories of his own father, what few memories he still had.

He recalled his father as being a steadfast rock, able to scare away boogiemen in closets and beneath beds, able to clean a scraped knee and cure it with a quick kiss... *He was predictable...* Ash recalled his father's lectures regarding the importance of good grades, of being honest and responsible, his lectures seeming to last for hours on end. As the father of a teenager *he was boring, dull.* Ash released an audible laugh into the empty room. *I've become my father. Predictable, boring, dull.*

He wondered if it was possible for his dad to provide support and guidance from the great beyond, serving as a mentor for Ash's pending journey. He was looking for his dad's help, instructing him as to how to be the good dad Ash so wanted to be. Ash did a playful slap to his jowls, bringing himself back to the reality of the task at hand and warding off the tears starting to build in his eyes. There were just too many changes in his life these days. When would it slow down? When would everything just be status quo again? ...When would his fear of criminal charges subside, his innocence proven. He was gripped with jarring bolt of fear. Was there incriminating evidence held in the two boxes from the office of the CFO?

He slid the top box from the stack and onto the floor before him. He removed the lid. Inside the white cardboard box, he found several picture frames. Ash recalled having seen them displayed on the corner of the Chief Financial Officer's desk on one of his few social visits to the impressive eighth floor office. The first photo was a professional headshot of Hillary Oakes, obviously taken during the honeymoon period. She was smiling. Another photo was of a young Kristen Oakes, dressed in riding gear with a thoroughbred standing patiently behind her. The final photo was of a beaming Bernie Oakes in loud plaid golf pants, holding the ball from the hole-in-one he had just made at the country club he once belonged to.

Ash found plaques that had hung on Bernie's office walls. A distinguished service award from PaseoParkTechnology, plaques of recognitions for his benevolent work in the Kansas City community, a certification in accounting issued from Wohlwend Hall. Other items were taken from his desktop and added to the box. His name plaque, a pencil holder possibly made by Krissy when she was a Girl Scout, a cut-crystal candy dish with a dozen or more wrapped peppermints strewn across the bottom of the almost empty box. Ash removed the final item, a coffee cup. He used his crooked index finger to lift it by its handle. The cup exhibited the stains of Bernie's last cup of coffee, a few dried grounds remaining stuck to the insides of the cup. Ash returned the items to the box and resituated its lid to shroud the mementos once again.

He started to pull the second box into his folded legs but stopped to bounce his knees in an attempt to restart the circulation of blood in his numbed extremities. He removed the lid to find the contents from the drawers of Bernie's desk. A monthly business journal rested on top with a multitude of file folders beneath, them containing documents now meaningless. Year-end reports, Five Year Projections, company newsletters. All the treeware was meaningless the second Bernard Oakes pulled the trigger on the .357 and decorated the study of his home with his brain.

Ashton Walker's eyes came to rest on a white #10 envelope tucked between two manila folders. The instant his fingers touched the thick mailer he knew what it was, what it contained. He felt his stomach take an upward heave, and he fought the progression of its contents, forcing the bile and his breakfast back downward. He had an instantaneous desire to tear up the envelope, to set it ablaze over the toilet, or to just deposit it in the building's trash chute, having never read its contents. A frightened inner voice told Ashton Walker he had found the suicide letter of Bernard Oakes.

Life was good. Why take the lid off of Pandora's box, possibly releasing all of the physical and emotional curses into the now happy lives of Kristen Oakes and himself? Why open the envelope? Maybe it wasn't even a suicide letter. Maybe it was a letter to another woman he was temporarily enthralled with. Wasn't it best to let the sleeping dog lie? Bernie was dead, he was gone. Why not continue to just move on? ...Why not know the exact reason or reasons he choose to end it all so abruptly? Why not learn where it all went wrong, where Bernie's life totally fell apart?

Ash heard his ringtone, the one specifically set for calls from Meredith. The sound was coming from the living room. He debated as to where he'd left his phone, either on the industrial cart or perhaps the cabinet containing his CD collection. He debated letting the call go to voice mail, to be returned after he had dealt with the letter. But instead he welcomed the diversion.

"Hey, Mere. What's up?" he wheezed.

"Is Krissy there?"

"No, she's out shopping with her mom for the baby. I can give her--."

"Good! I want to throw a bridal/baby shower for her. Well, for you guys. I need to know who to put on the guest list."

"Oh, jeez… She, she really doesn't have any friends other than Hillary." Ash did a quick search of his brain for names of people she talked to on a frequent basis and discovered there were no names that came immediately to mind. "She went to college in the East and had sorority sisters, but they're all over the country."

"How about high school friends still here in KC?"

"I…I…" Ash flopped onto the sofa. "She's never really talked about anyone and I don't think her high school days were all that enjoyable for her. She just kind of floated through the hallways, graduated and moved on." He realized he had done much the same thing. Maybe they really were two peas in a pod.

"Well see if you can come up with a potential guest list in a roundabout way and let me know."

With an embarrassed laugh, "I guess our entire circle of friends reside here in the Old Folks Home."

"You could do much worse. At least you're not giving me a list of the guys on your cellblock."

"Bye, Mere…"

Stalling, Ash went to the kitchen and fished a beer from the refrigerator. He poured it into a heavy mug and took it with him, back to the empty bedroom. The envelope still laid where he had left it on the dingy carpet. Easing himself to the floor, careful not to spill the beer, he then scooted to rest his back against the wall. Taking a sizeable swig of the cold beer and closing his eyes, he forced himself to open the envelope.

His fingers trembled as he removed the trifold stationery from its berth. He opened it, counting four page covered front and back, from the top margin to the bottom, single spaced, and written in the meticulous handwriting of an accountant. Ash began reading the letter, addressed to Norman Roland, Chief Executive Officer, PaseoParkTechnology.

Bernard Oakes delivered his opening statement, a reminiscent recounting of his twenty-two-year career with PaseoParkTechnology. He wrote of a time when he had ethics and standards, a time when he traveled a moral high ground and conducted business in a like fashion. And then came the time when the high ground began to give way beneath his feet, him surrounded by people without scruples, governed by avarice. And so too came the decline of his own self-control and principles.

The letter attested to the regret of Bernard Oakes for his inability to standup to those that either saw nothing wrong in their actions or just chose to look the other way. He berated himself for following the same dirty and disgusting path of greed and debauchery set forth by the brotherhood of the eighth floor. He went on to highlight specific incidents of underhanded dealings, naming names, pointing his finger and assigning responsibility for the misdeeds.

He outlined in great detail the deceitful construction and execution of dealings not only within PaseoParkTechnology but with both competitors and those thought to be comrades in the industry. In an obvious moment of deep regret and guilt, he confessed his part in many of these despicable deeds. He stated that it was too late to wash his own hands or to step away from his hideous actions, but he refused to continue on the same deplorable path. He saw no other way to end the travesty but to call out those involved and for he, himself, to take the path ending his own life.

Nearing the end of the four-page edict Ashton Walker read his own name. He snapped to his knees, knocking over the beer mug and saturating a patch of the dirty carpet with what remained in the mug. The letter, now just inches from his face, provided confirmation that he, himself, was being groomed to follow that very same path of corruption. He felt his chest constricting in panic, a suppressed urge to cry out in fear was muffled in his throat. He quickly turned the page to continue reading about those situations he had been consulted on, his solicited input certain to earn Ashton Walker at least twenty, maybe even thirty years behind bars in a federal prison. *Why had he ever told Bernie Oakes how to legally do the illegal? Was he looking for the man's approval, his respect? Was he looking for acceptance into the eighth-floor fold?*

The tears were now unfettered, the sound of his uncontrollable sobbing filled the soon-to-be nursery. He felt compelled to run, to hide, but to where? Had he really done anything wrong? What was his crime? Being stupid, being gullible... being blinded by a false sense of belonging at the popular kid's table? He rose to his feet, turning the page over as his eyes rushedly took in the concluding testimony of Bernard Oakes.

He came to the final paragraph. He fitfully skimmed the words. He reread the words, questioning what he was seeing. As he read it a third time, painstakingly word by word, he felt his knees give way and his body collapse to the dingy carpet. An avalanche of what could only be described as blissful relief usurped his entire being.

Bernard Oakes' final paragraph contained a declaration of Ashton Walker's noninvolvement in any wrong doing. Bernard Oakes provided exculpatory evidence, supporting the innocence of Ashton Walker. The CFO provided irrefutable evidence that Ashton Walker was never a knowing or willing participant in the despicable dealings of PaseoParkTechnology. Ashton Walker had never given any firm directives, made any of the duplicitous decisions, or carried out any of the crimes. He was nothing more than a pawn for those on the eight-floor to do the unthinkable.

The four pages came to rest on the floor next to Ash as he wrapped his arms around his knees and rocked in a search for comfort. He used his open palms to futilely remove the flow of tears from his cheeks. He looked to the ceiling, giving thanks for this final act of Bernard Oakes to clear Ash's name of any wrongdoing. *How could he have been so stupid, so easily manipulated, so played. Why?*

Yes, why? Why in Hell would a lowly lawyer be included in the inner circle of the Eighth-floor Good Old Boys of PaseoParkTechnology, going on a weekend drinking binge in Chicago, Illinois? Why would someone like him be included in lunches and happy hours with those in power and in control of the billion-dollar enterprise? Why was he even being considered for a throne on the eight floor of the tech giant when he had never shown any interest or aptitude for such a position? *Why?*

Why? Bernard Oakes had brought the inner circle a sacrificial lamb but had a change of heart and saved that lamb before the dagger could slit Ash's throat. Ash was nothing more than a fall guy.

Ash scribbled a note to Krissy: *Something came up at the office. I'll be home ASAP.* He left the note on the dining room table where she'd see it upon her return home. He jumped into his car, calling Matt on his way, telling him to meet him at Trailblazers for a drink with a side order of scandal.

Was Trailblazers a good place? Would anyone from the Chicago contingency be there to overhear his side of the conversation? What did Ash care? They were all going down, everyone on the Chi town jaunt had been named in the letter. A post script, included at the end of Bernard Oakes' suicide letter, informed the CEO that the original of the letter had been delivered to the FBI that same morning. Uncle Bernie had made two copies of the original: one for the Norman Roland, one for himself.

"Damn," Matt whispered, refolding the letter and putting it back into hiding in its white envelope. He tossed the envelope back at Ash with the same energy if the envelope had contained anthrax.

"I'm blown away by this one! I, I don't know what to make of it." Ash tucked the envelope back inside the inner pocket of his windbreaker.

"So what did Krissy say?"

"She wasn't home when I found the letter. I . . . I don't know that I'm going to show her the letter."

"Why not? It's her uncle, and at least he had a turn of good conscience at the end. He might have just saved your butt, too, Junior. Then again, you could still be in big trouble if any of those clowns is working on a plea deal and trying to use you as their personal scapegoat."

"Gee thanks. I've been living on antiacids for almost a month now, my stomach has been in such a knot. I was hoping this letter would totally clear my name... Bernie just had a change of heart. He fully intended to make me a sacrificial lamb, but I think he saw how much Krissy loves me. He couldn't do that to her." Ash finished his beer and debated ordering another. "Yeah, Bernie may be family, but I think Krissy already has enough bad memories of him that she doesn't need to add any more."

"It's your call." Matt took a swig of his craft brew. "I'm surprised the FBI hasn't contacted you. Maybe they've got more than they need with the info Bernie provided to them. Maybe they've been watching PaseoParkTechnology all along. But seems they would want you to be a corroborating witness to firm up their case."

Ash signaled the waitress with his raised glass. He looked at the few other faces that had taken cover in the barroom on a Saturday morning. What were they hiding from? What deep dark secrets had they discovered? Ash instructed his fingertips to massage his throbbing temples, his eyes tightly closed. Matt and Ash sat across from each other in silence, each processing the events of the past and speculating on the events to come as a result.

"I need to settle my tab." He flipped his credit card at the waitress as she placed the fresh beer in front of him. Returning his attention to Matt, "I wouldn't mind helping to take down PaseoParkTechnology all the way to bedrock. Doug told me last week that BT2.0 had picked up another four PPT clients, big ones. Now I think I know why. The best part is those four accounts are bringing enough business that Bryant is going to be hiring fourteen new positions."

"I think that's just going to be the tip of the iceberg. BT2.0 could very well make PPT look like small change in the tech industry if we play this right." Matt finished off the last of the beer in his glass.

"I'm thinking another attorney, maybe two more are going to be needed real soon. Are you interested in a promotion? Maybe Doug can have your door retitled: *Director of Legal Affairs*."

Matt pushed his empty glass to the center of the table. He snidely looked at his boss. "I've always wanted to have an affair, not necessarily a legal one."

"Just not with my future wife." Ash scored game point. With a two-finger salute to Matt, he headed for the front the door of Trailblazers.

Chapter 30

Consistent Spontaneity

A new tradition had been initiated each evening in Unit 3B. Before turning out the light on the ebony ledge of the king-size bed, Ash and Krissy flipped a coin to see who the early riser would be the next morning in response to either the coos or loud wails of Draven James Walker. The three-week-old infant had decided to make an early appearance into the world, delaying the best laid plans of his parents to get married in the Johnson County Courthouse on that same Tuesday morning.

Draven… Another name taken from a character on a television sitcom, keeping the trailer park tradition alive in the lineage of Walker men.

"I'm up." Krissy mumbled from beneath her pillow in response to the brouhaha coming from the nursery just down the hall.

"I won the toss last night. I've got him." Ash rolled on to his stomach in hopes the crying infant would suddenly decide a cold wet diaper wasn't so bad after all.

"I've got a busy day today and I need to get started." She brought her feet to the floor, sliding them into her waiting flipflops. "I've got this."

"It's Saturday. What have you got to do today?" Ash mumbled as he resituated his pillow in preparation for his return to dreamland,

"You'll see Ashton Walker. You will see."

With a yawn and a stretch, she then waddled from the master bedroom, still a little tender from delivering a seven-pound baby. But, she most definitely had things to do today! She entered the nursery and scooped up the infant who gurgled with delight at having a morning visitor capable of alleviating his current discomforts.

"Draven James, we have a very exciting day today! Let's get you a clean diaper and a bottle, and then get you into your tux."

Krissy wrapped the baby in a light blanket and took him onto the living room balcony to enjoy the morning sunshine along with what remained of the bottle of pumped milk. A glance at her watch confirmed it was 9:04 a.m.. She took her cellphone from the pocket of her hoodie and speed dialed Ash's sister's number.

Meredith answered on the second ring. "Morning Krissy! Everything is ready on my part! Your mom is already there to meet the florist. She said Matt and Hilly just arrived and are doing whatever else on your list still needs to be done. Does Ash suspect anything?"

"Not anything that I can tell. Then again he's such a typical male, oblivious to most any change in the routine. And now with Draven, we no longer have *any* routine."

"Well, he's getting what he deserves! He has always loved your ability to surprise him. This should really do it! We'll see you in a couple of hours. Oh! And don't forget to bring the license and the rings!"

"Oh my God! Thank you for the reminder! I just have to find where Ash put them for safe keeping."

Krissy continued her morning. She'd take an occasional peek in at the sleeping attorney as she fussed with her hair and makeup with more painstaking effort than usual. She spied the matching wedding bands in their small velveteen box on top of one of the tool chest dressers in the master bedroom. Ash began to stir as the clock approached 10:00, kicking the covers from his body.

"Thanks for letting me sleep in. I owe you big time."

"No worries. It's an awesome day. Let's take Draven for a stroller ride in the park this morning."

"Sounds good. Let me get a shower and some breakfast and we can head out."

"No rush but be quick." She started to leave him to his ritual adding, "Wear something nice. Maybe your navy chinos and that new shirt I bought you a few weeks ago."

"The one for the courthouse? Isn't an oxford button-down a little dressy for a walk in a park?"

"Maybe, but I just want to see how handsome you look in it."

"For you? Anything."

As the morning continued, Krissy took fleeting glances at the clock in the kitchen, the watch on her wrist, and the digital numbers on the nightstand as she changed her own clothes. She put on the new sundress and the cute sandals she had purchased just for this day. She gave the final touches to her hair and makeup, taking a purposeful glance in the full-length mirror on the back of the master bathroom's door. She frowned at the smidge of baby weight remaining on her abdomen. She called to Ash, when all the clocks reported 10:40 a.m.

"Ready?"

"Just about. Are we on some sort of schedule here? You're like a pinball, bouncing from one thing to another."

"Maybe. Maybe not."

Ash took his favorite baseball cap from the guest closet. Krissy started to challenge his choice but decided to let it slide, giving him a "huff" and then a "never mind." But, when Ash looked into the baby carriage he realized something was in the works.

"A tuxedo onesie? Seriously?"

"He rocks it, doesn't he?"

"What's going on? You're gorgeous, more so than usual. Our son is in a tuxedo. I'm dressed like I'm going to church." His eyes brightened. "What have you planned?"

"Can't we look nice for a change? Do we always have to look like we just checked out from a thrift store?"

"When have *you* ever shopped in a secondhand store?"

"Umm?" She fostered a pensive look. "Halloween when I was in college. You can make a great costume with some of their stuff."

With Draven in his carriage, the couple left their condo and headed for the elevator to the first floor. Ash noted the hallway was particularly quite this morning, the blaring of Betty Stubbs's television was absent. *Was Betty not well? Was her television broken?* The pungent odor of aftershaves and perfumes was unusually prevalent, more so than usual, in the elevator this morning as they rode downward. Ash fanned his hand above Draven's tiny nose in an attempt to bring untainted air to the infant's lungs.

They left the building, cautiously rolling the buggy down the dip in the sidewalk and onto the asphalt of the horseshoe driveway. The family of three maneuvered towards the intersection visible from their living room balcony and crossed the street to the public park. A more perfect day with its blue sky, pleasant temperature, and low humidity was atypical for this time of year in Kansas City.

Krissy took quick glances towards the waiting pavilion. She heard the sounds of conversations and laughter that Ash had yet to notice. That was until he spied all of the large bows of white netting and silver ribbons tied to the surrounding trees leading up the path to the pavilion and nearby gazebo.

"Hmm, I wonder if someone's getting married today? Look at all these big bows."

"I don't know Ashton Walker. It would seem like it with all of those white bows, and all of those people under the pavilion looking at us."

Ash stopped in his tracks. His eyes took attendance of the faces looking back at him. "Krissy…?"

"Ashton Walker?"

Vi Fabick's booming voice called out, "If anyone objects to Ash and Krissy getting married, speak now or FOREVER hold your peace!" A chorus of "Hear! Hear!" followed along with applause and cheers.

Ash and Krissy scanned the open pavilion, nary an inch of the structure remaining uncovered. There was white netting with arrangements of flowers and greenery creatively interspersed on every support pillar. The long picnic tables were covered in white table cloths with centerpieces of blue hydrangeas and white spider mums. And dressed in their Sunday best were the residents of Parc LeMay, the employees and significant others of Bryant Technology 2.0 and the staff and a few clients of Krissy's not-for-profit.

"Our marriage license is only good for thirty days, bucko. It was now or never." Krissy gave Ash the spirited hardnose look that had recently come to replace her solicitous head tilt and lecherous tongue scan. The hardened look came into play in those situations where the "take charge" in Krissy superseded the manipulative maneuvering of the nymph. She knew how to use both techniques to her advantage to get the job done and procure what she desired at the time.

A woman's voice was heard from the nearby gazebo. "Ash and Krissy, I'm Reverend Martha Holt from First United Methodist Church. It is my honor to officiate this ceremony if it is indeed your wish to join in holy matrimony."

The reality of the situation began to infiltrate Ash's level of comprehension. Spontaneous. Unpredictable. Endearing. Kristin Louise Oakes was everything Ashton Walker had ever dreamed of, hoped for, even prayed for. He surveyed the surrounding scene, savoring what was taking place, ready and willing to go forward with the life altering event being offered to them by the minister.

"Reverend Holt, where would you like for us to stand?" Ash joyously called back to the woman in her long black robe and colorful stole. Two other people, Hillary Oakes and Matt Blaylock already stood waiting on each side of the minister.

As if on cue, Ash's father's Glenn Miller CD could be heard, the opening notes of *Moonlight Serenade* filling the pavilion. Krissy moved into Ash's arms, again ignoring his personal space.

"I know you said no first dance, but we've already done that—" A wail was heard from Draven Walker across the pavilion, "amongst a few other things. But, all good things always come to an end. We just need to leave good memories for whoever remains behind."

"Dance with me, Kristin Walker. Let's make some good memories."

THE END

Made in the USA
Las Vegas, NV
26 April 2023